CHILD OF WINTER
Ten Dark and Twisted Tales

CHILD OF WINTER
Ten Dark and Twisted Tales

T.R. Hitchman

CORONA
BOOKS

First published in the United Kingdom in 2016

by Corona Books UK
www.coronabooks.com

An earlier version of 'The Homecoming' was
previously published as an e-book by
Spinetinglers Publishing 2014

ISBN 978-0-9932472-3-1

Cover star Rozzy Perring
photographed by Catherine Bignold

Cover design by Colourburst
www.colourburst.com

CONTENTS

The Homecoming	9
Tell Me	49
The Eye of the Beholder	57
Bricks and Mortar	69
The Stranger You Know	79
Child of Winter	88
Every Queen Deserves a King	112
You Were Always on My Mind	123
Calaveritas	129
The Dead	144

Human madness is oftentimes a cunning and most feline thing. When you think it fled, it may have but become transfigured into some still subtler form.

Herman Melville, *Moby Dick*

The Homecoming

I

She gritted her teeth, hissing in slithers of cold air. The peculiar mewing, which she had first thought came from some lost or injured animal, had come from her own mouth. She tried to stop it. It had been as involuntary as breathing, and it now seemed too quiet. Her legs were as shaky and feeble as a newly born calf, and she had a sudden urge to crouch down. She studied the ground, which was peppered with a thin, crisp layer of light snow, the first of the season. She hoped that the pain, which now flooded over her in brief but regular waves, would subside.

She had woken that morning wet and perspiring. The room was still dark, and the dawn was only just teasing over the horizon. A good hour or more before morning. She wondered if she had been dreaming as her bedclothes were coiled around her, as if she'd been fighting some imaginary monster. She had once been told that the dreams you remembered were the ones that you had only moments before waking. She supposed that her nightmare had occurred hours ago and it was something else that had woken her out of her troubled sleep.

She had dreamt a lot lately, mostly about her father. In her dreams Pa's face was slightly blurred, but she recognised the hands. The nails bitten down and knuckles calloused, the hands of a man who had worked out in all weathers. It was those hands she missed the most. They had lifted her up as a child and led her across the fields for most of her infant and adolescent life.

For weeks now she had been waking at this time. Strange lost moments when the night and morning were slowly colliding. She could not hear Ma yet. That familiar clatter of pans and the gentle moaning that Ma supposed was in her head but escaped through pursed lips. She closed her eyes, knowing full well that sleep would not come. Her mind was too alive. It raced with thoughts that wouldn't be abated even though she willed them to. Eventually she couldn't bear it any longer and stumbled in the twilight, glad to feel the familiar shiver as she cautiously crept across the room. She'd been pouring water into the wash bowl when the pain had gripped her. She had dropped the jug and had stood for a few moments in the pool of icy water. She listened then, supposing that the crash would have woken Ma up, but the house remained silent. She was frightened to move at first, fearing that even the smallest of steps would send that sharp and unforgiving pain through her stomach. Eventually she did move, cautiously stepping forward and was thankful that she felt nothing at all.

She had supposed then that the baby was on its way.

She remembered the annual lambing every spring. The fields still cold, but there had always been that impending feeling in the air that better weather was on its way. The sky bright and full of the hope that summer and its warm, long days were nearly in reach. Pa led the way. He would whisper gently soothing words to her as he felt her body become tense. It was the ewes that frightened her. Their strangled cries, eyes wide and pleading or so it seemed to her innocent eyes. But her father had pushed his hand through her hair and told her not to be afraid. The pain, he promised, was a temporary thing. It would soon pass and there would be lambs at the end of it.

He was right. Gradually with each passing spring she coped better with the awful sight of seeing the ewes in such agony. Instead, she would gawk in wonder as each lamb came out with an uncivilised plop on to the straw beneath. A mass of bloody discharge and flaying limbs. Every time she would wait with bated breath and let out a relived sigh when the little things started to bleat and the ewes instinctively turned their heads to study their new born.

The pain had quickly subsided. She hoped that the child, the one she had swaddled under layers of skirts uncomfortably through the summer months, would wait a while. She had wished for her father, to feel that familiar hold on her shoulders and be as soothing as he was to those poor ewes. She knew she had to be strong, but the thought of Pa brought tears to her eyes and she hadn't quite enough strength to prevent them from falling.

She felt wetness and stared with a fearful horror at the ground beneath her opened legs. She had expected to see blood, but to her relief and confusion there was nothing but a wet patch, which appeared to wash away the day's attempt at snow. Then suddenly another bolt of pain and she cried out, looking up hesitantly, supposing her cry was so loud that Ma would be alerted and she'd see her emerging shape in the distance somewhere. Another spasm of pain quickly followed, but she was more prepared for this one and she clenched hard. Instead of a cry she let out a deep moan. The pain struck again, and a sudden need to push became as natural as breathing itself. She realised now there was nothing she could do to control it. Instead, she let her body take over and she followed each desire it made, as if it were a separate thing and no longer part of her.

And it told her to keep on pushing.

When the baby did finally arrive it was so quick that she looked down and gasped at the sight of the naked mottled little body beneath her. She tried to think back to those lambs, of their sudden jerky movements. That natural desire to escape from their glutinous sack and get up, walk around.

The baby didn't move. It lay curled up, as if anticipating some kind of attack. She cautiously put her hand down, but withdrew it quickly, frightened of what her touch would do. She tried again, this time letting the tips of her fingers caress the small fragile arm. It didn't stir, and she pulled her hand away.

It happened on the farm sometimes. One of the lambs came out like a heavy weight and she had supposed that it was dead. But her Pa would take this unmoving lamb into his arms, wiping away the sticky remains of birth, rubbing it so vigorously that she was fearful that he might do it more harm than good. But it was as if Pa caused a miracle, because the lamb would start to struggle and eventually have enough strength to attempt to escape from out of his arms, bleating for its mother before he was forced to put it back down on the straw. There the ewe would nuzzle and push it towards her, oblivious to the fact that she had almost lost one of her offspring.

She gathered the small body up into her arms, just as Pa had done with one of those lambs, attempting to do the same. She wasn't as rough though, she hadn't quite got his confidence, but she moved quickly up and down the body, hoping to see a small sign, a twitch, something to give her a bit of hope.

But she knew that not all the lambs lived.

She had laid the baby back on the ground and it appeared strangely content. Its eyes so tightly shut she wondered whether it had made the decision not to open them long before it had been released from within her.

The cry came out. It was as instinctive as the need to push and just as unexpected. She lifted up her hand and traced the solitary tear and its path down her cheek, catching it before it fell off the edge. So many times had she wished the child was gone. Now she would do anything in the world to hear its cries, to press its cold little body into her own and hear the steady beats of its heart.

She got up quickly, and suddenly couldn't bear to look at it. Instead, she took off her shawl and wrapped the child up, though she could still feel the cold of its still little body through the rough wool. It was a lump of nothing on the ground, a blot on an otherwise perfect sheet of white. She turned, walked slowly back to the farmhouse, turning back only once to stare in bewilderment at the small mound.

Ma had glanced up at her when she had returned, glared down at her daughter's belly, noting how her daughter held herself tightly, looking up and seeing the tear stained face.

'It's for the best,' Ma had hissed and had turned back to the dishes as if she had lost nothing more than a button.

It was after her and Ma had had supper and there was still a little light left of the day that she thought of it, out there in the fields. She felt a twinge of guilt and supposed she should have buried it. It deserved that, if nothing else. Ma had looked at her with suspicion when she went towards the door.

'Why are you going out, it's getting dark?'

She noted the quiver in her Ma's voice and the reason behind it. 'Just for a moment Ma, not for long,' she replied.

Her mother smiled, but it was tight, like it cost her those half pennies she'd been saving and thought her daughter knew nothing about.

It was dark when she returned and she was chilled to

the bone. She had searched and searched, thinking she must be mistaken about where she had left the baby.

But her boy had gone.

That night it was the cries of ewes that haunted her dreams. They cried out, it seemed, for a lamb lost out in the blackness somewhere.

II

The weatherman had promised snow, but it hadn't come. Instead, the sky remained a dull grey, heavy with cloud and the chill, which had hung in the air for days and had a habit of seeping into flesh and chilling the bones beneath, had lessened a little. Constance stared out at the fields. This time of year it looked so bleak, the earth a farmer's nightmare, hard and unyielding. Everything was dead. Fossils of the frosty mornings. At least the snow would have covered it up, have made it looked almost pretty. Constance pulled her coat tighter around herself, but she continued to shiver. In her old age she felt the sharp edge of the December air. Lately though, it crawled deeper than her skin and remained there. Constance would lie in bed and wonder if this damn winter would ever end and she'd get to feel the warmth of the sun again before she died.

It didn't help there was no sun today. Not that it offered much in the way of heat when it did come out, but it bathed everything in light and the land beneath oozed a kind of gratefulness for those brief respites in the otherwise long, drab hours. Today the twilight seemed to have stretched from late morning, but now the day was coming to a true close. The fields and farm were bathed in an eerie glow. It was now that Constance could see them come.

The ghosts.

Pa, his cap pushed firmly over his face, the collar turned up seemingly inadequate against the wind, which blew determinedly against him. He never did seem to feel the cold. At first glance it appeared he was grimacing, but Constance knew that, in fact, it was a smile. He loved his kingdom. He knew every inch of the land, the fields and each hedgerow, which had grown alongside him as he had grown from boy to man. The farm had been passed down each generation, and it was to continue with her brother. He was as he had been, caught forever in the age that she had known him as a young woman. Constance couldn't imagine him an old man, and she found a peculiar comfort in the fact that fate had taken that out of his hands.

Sometimes the spectre was her brother Samuel. He was so recognisable from his familiar stride. A walk of determination, as if he were marching to a war, that's what Ma would say. He'd been that way since they lost Pa. That careless gait of a boy replaced by that of the man who had realised the weight of responsibility that suddenly rested on his shoulders.

He walked with that same resolve on the day he left, and, even though Constance had called out his name, he didn't look round once and kept on walking across the fields, to the gate, until he was nothing but a speck of blurred colour, and within a blink he was gone.

Later on that fateful day, when it had grown dark and Samuel did not return, Ma had questioned her over and over. Ever since Pa's death she'd had the clinging insecurity that one day she'd lose another one of them. Ma paced the kitchen anxiously, her hands scrunching up the fabric of her apron into tight balls, darting quizzical looks at her daughter. Constance had squirmed with discomfort, wondering if Ma could see through her. She chewed her lip till she tasted blood, and the resulting sting every time she passed the tip of her tongue over it was a kind of self-punishment.

Constance watched her mother constantly in the days that followed. Her conscience eager to see change, to see her Ma accepting that her first born had gone for good. But a creak or noise that sounded like an opened door and Ma's eyes would dart up, ready to chastise and welcome back her son in equal measures. Most days she was like a dog waiting patiently by its master's side, begging for scraps. Constance found it pathetic and uncomfortable to watch.

It had been a good many years since Ma had passed away, but Constance still felt the guilt as fresh as if it were yesterday.

She knew that Samuel was never coming back, but over the years she indulged herself with a fantasy that perhaps he would, of course as an old man. Lately though, it was the mound of earth she pictured, with her shawl still carefully arranged over the small body. In her mind she'd be walking towards it, slow and cautiously, ignoring the small voice inside that screamed out it wasn't real, that it couldn't be.

And then there was the recurring dream. In it, Constance was standing over that pitiful grave and had plucked up enough courage to pull back the shawl. To her horror, it wasn't the baby at all but a small lamb, bloody and lifeless. She would wake up her throat painful and dry, like she'd been screaming.

Constance thought about the child now she was long past bearing any more, nursing her grief like it was a baby itself. A living breathing thing, its small hands grasping hold of her. It was a boy; she did know that. So, in her head, was this child with tightly curled blond hair. A family trait, passed to each male child of her family.

Constance would hold her pillow to her chest and imagine that the soft downy feathers breathed, that deep among them was that small heart, beating steady and regularly next to her own. Once upon a time she felt the urge to howl out in pain and was forced to push her face into that same pillow so that her cries were muted. Constance ever wondered if Ma heard those peculiar muffled outbursts, or saw her red rimmed eyes and the dark shadows which accompanied them in the morning. But if she did, she never once commented. Now there was no one to hear them, but oddly the tears wouldn't come. Like she'd cried them all out.

The house remained a stilted silence for years after. The air so heavy with loss that Constance wondered how the pair of them could breathe. But loss was peculiar; it pushed down, forced itself so deep it was out of view. Of course it remained there, simmering like a stew. Constance's gnawed at her insides, eating away at the fat in her body, making her fleshless and wiry, wrists so thin they gave the impression they would break. Her mother, on the other hand, fed hers, clothes that had fitted now strained over rolls of flesh and bloated thighs, and buttons constantly threatened to burst. They were an odd pairing, two opposites, united only in their own private and unspoken grief.

Constance looked up. Today it was Samuel's ghost that appeared to be striding towards her. She strained her eyes, hoping that the image she carried always in her head was the one she saw approaching her now. And yes, the figure walking towards her was the Samuel she always remembered, that stride, purposely marching and, in Constance's mind, back to the place he had run away from all that time ago.

Constance waited patiently for him to gradually fade, a

mirage that would disperse into the mist of the wintery late afternoon.

But the figure kept on striding towards her. A body that was solid and real. Soon becoming a body that was very solid and as real as her own.

III

Constance shut her eyes. Her mouth was trembling, and the sensation crawled slowly down, right to her toes. In her heart she knew it wasn't Samuel walking towards her. Not her Samuel. Constance supposed her time had come. But she thought it a cruel God that bought her own brother seemingly back from the dead to take her to Hell, as she supposed that was where she was heading. And yet there was no better person Constance could have wished for, to keep her company on her last journey.

On opening her eyes again, she found that the figure was continuing to walk towards her. Constance felt less afraid. In the last few years she had known that death wasn't far around the corner. She was an old woman and this seemed a more fitting end than that poor Pa had. Or even Ma, curled up in that lonely cold bed, in pain, fearing the inevitable.

Constance had often thought over the years what she would have said to her brother if he ever returned. In those early weeks and months her emotions rocked from anger and disappointment to sadness and the desperate need to see him again. When she was angry she attacked each one of her jobs on the farm with a violent enthusiasm. She was thankful that the work was not of a delicate nature, such as that of a seamstress or nurse, as she would have done more harm than good to a dainty piece of silk or a patient's wound.

Constance was angry because he had left her here with Ma. When Pa had died she had taken a comforting back seat. The farm was Samuel's responsibility, as was Ma for that matter. But when he walked away he had dumped the whole sorry mess into her lap. Constance became a prisoner. The fields were her yard, the hedgerows were the walls and Ma her gaoler. Constance carried the burden as if it were chains, and sometimes it felt just as heavy.

In the times when she was filled with sadness at his loss, mourning him just as much as she mourned Pa, she clung as desperately as Ma did to the idea that he was alive somewhere. On the scant occasions she did leave the farm to visit the nearby village she searched fervently. On market day especially, Constance surveyed the crowds, hoping to see the familiar head of blond curly hair. There were many times when she thought she had. Once in particular Constance had followed a man she took to be her brother for several minutes, and managed to finally catch up with him. She had grabbed his arm, and could not hide the disappointment when she was greeted with the face of a stranger. The man hadn't failed to notice how upset Constance had appeared, so he had offered to take her to the local public house. But he had taken Constance's hand in such a way it suggested that he had every intention of using the young woman's distress very much to his advantage. Constance had quickly apologised, and had prised herself away from the man's suddenly keen and overbearing grip.

The months that followed were hard. Once it had dawned on Ma that Samuel was not returning she became angry and disillusioned. And, of course, the only person whom she could focus this anger on was her daughter. Constance quickly realised she could do nothing right. Her best was never quite what Samuel could do. It grew worse when the mild autumn turned into one of the worst winters the pair had ever seen, even worse than the one in which Pa had died. Constance was up so early that there were some days it felt she had not slept at all. Many of the livestock died. Several good sheep used for breeding were lost in a blizzard that was so fierce you were unable to see in front of you. There was another where she and Ma were trapped in the house for a couple of days. Both of them like caged lionesses, pacing around each other, teeth bared and ready to attack if given half the chance.

Constance carried on, though. It would be too easy to abandon it all like her brother had. She found a perverse satisfaction in trying to prove Ma wrong. It got her through each day, forced her up in the mornings when she would have preferred to keep her eyes closed and hope that the darkness that existed underneath those closed lids would swallow her whole. Of course, her grief lay under the surface; no matter how hard she worked the pain continued to weep like an open wound. But Constance learned to live with it. That ache, the one which had gripped her when she had laid her shawl over that cold little body, remained, but it was like her heartbeat, steady and unvarying. In the end Ma criticised her a little less, but Constance supposed it was more to do with old age having the effect of smoothing away Ma's temper, than the fact she was finally doing something right.

The man was near. Near enough for Constance to realise that this was no spirit from the other world, or the ghost of her brother, but real flesh and blood. He was dressed smartly, a suit like that her brother and Pa would only wear for best or a special occasion. Certainly not suitable for the weather or for someone who was used to working the land. He had turned the collar of his jacket up, and the tie beneath kept on escaping. It flapped about in the breeze like a piece of loose skin. His shoes also were inadequate, and now the highly polished surface only remained on the tops of them. He was grimacing, but this was no disguised smile like Pa's. He wasn't used to walking out in weather like this, and the displeasure he wore very clearly on his face. He was concentrating hard on trying to reach where she stood, and Constance wished she'd been right about it being just a ghost.

The man unexpectedly broke out into a smile. 'Hello,' he called out, and then repeated himself, presuming by the blank expression on Constance's face that she hadn't heard him the first time around. He carried on walking towards her, regardless of the fact that she had yet to utter a word to him.

'You're on private land.' Constance finally spoke in a faltering tone, but it appeared the man didn't hear what she said.

'God, I'm glad to see somebody. It's felt as if I've been walking for miles ... not exactly dressed for the occasion.' He gave a nervous chuckle, shaking his head comically. 'Really out in the sticks aren't you?' he continued, ignoring her initial statement, and there was a slight nervousness to his tone, perhaps he sensed her unease and he continued to smile.

'I thought you were somebody else,' Constance hissed, supposing the stranger hadn't heard her.

'Oh... really, look I'm sorry to, well, trespass like this, but...' He shrugged his shoulders, the expression even more strained.

Constance could see he was shivering, stamping his feet up and down in a failed attempt to keep himself warm. 'You'll catch your death dressed like that. My Pa did.' She pulled her own coat tighter around her as if to emphasise the point.

'I'll only take a moment of your time, I promise ... please, I'm in bit of fix.' He was shuffling on the spot, his chin lowered so it almost rested on his chest.

Constance remembered how Samuel would do such a thing as a boy, especially when he was in trouble with Ma. For some reason Ma couldn't resist it, shaking her head as if exasperated with her own weakness. Constance felt just the same now. Samuel had a way, a boyish charm that remained even as a man of nineteen. The man appeared to have such a skill. 'You better follow me,' she said, 'as long as you're not long, mind.'

The man smiled even more keenly, if that were possible. Constance had not seen such a smile for a good many years.

IV

The man stood awkwardly in the hallway. He seemed out of place here. The sharp lines of his shirt and tie jarred with the soft, blurred shabby edges of her home. Constance had lived in its chaos for so long she had come to suppose there was nothing wrong with it at all. But now, with this stranger standing in front of her, she looked about the place with fresh eyes.

The farm house appeared to ooze dirt, dust and grime from every crevice. As if it perspired and shredded its old skin like some kind of reptile. When Ma had died Constance neglected the well-practised routine. It was as if one day she had looked around and realised that a certain point of no return had been passed, and no amount of scrubbing and polishing would clear it. But also there was something comforting about the filth. The mail unopened and layered like an elaborate wedding cake on the table, which once upon a time they all ate around. The hallway had the remnants of each passing season, mud from the wet spring dried and dark like chocolate, and there was a scattering of leaves blown in from the autumnal breeze which announced the end of summer. There were even remnants of wool, probably fallen from a boot. A sad memory of the livestock Constance once had and which had been at times, it seemed, a willing ear to listen to her. There was even a flower dried up and brown, snatched from the fields during the summer months, perhaps late evening when it was still warm.

'Shall I shut the door?' he said. 'Don't want to let the heat out.'

She noticed his shoulders were still hunched. Constance had got used to the chill of the place. There were times when she rarely took her coat off. The man was taking it all in, trying his best to be as subtle as possible, and Constance wondered what he was comparing it to. 'I don't get many visitors now,' she murmured. It was the truth, but coming out of her mouth it felt like an excuse, and she felt ashamed about the state she was living in.

'Ah don't worry, it's... homely,' he said with an obvious awkwardness.

Luckily, she had lit the fire in the front room, but it was quite pathetic and spluttering, and the sudden gust from the opened door had threatened to quash it completely. Constance wished that she had put some extra coals on it that morning. The only suitable chair was in the corner, her father's, the oily imprint of his head still there. It had stood untouched since his death, a layer of dust scattered over its surface like the snow they had promised. Constance grabbed both its arms, but hadn't quite realised what a solid bit of furniture it was.

'Let me help, please,' said the man, who was behind her suddenly, and she flinched to find he was closer than anticipated.

He had gripped the chair and their hands were almost touching. Constance quickly pulled hers away. She didn't like the contrast of her mottled wrinkled skin, thin and yellowing like parchment compared to his smooth hands. The nails were milky white, neatly cut, the fingers delicate and spindly, almost like a woman's. Constance had not seen hands like that in her lifetime. The hands that had lifted her up as a child, that had taken her own in theirs, were calloused and rough like sandpaper, blushed red from the wind.

'Let me,' he said. 'Good sturdy chair eh? Don't make them like this anymore.'

The chair had been in the house before Constance had been born; perhaps it had been a wedding gift to her parents. The man stood back up and studied his hands, wiped the dust on his trousers. He sat down, kneeling forward to get what warmth he could from the fire.

'The phone is in the hallway.' Constance bit her lip awkwardly. It was under a layer of papers, she was sure. She rarely used it. There was no one to ring.

'Oh, right. Do you mind if I just sit here a while, just get a bit of warmth back into these fingers of mine?' He looked eagerly up, rubbing his hands over and over again.

Perhaps because she hadn't had company for such a long while, Constance hadn't the heart to say no.

'I better introduce myself,' he continued. 'My name's William, William Barnes.' And then he waited.

'Constance,' she whispered.

'Well, Constance, do you live here alone? No family?'

Constance shook her head. She'd been alone for some time now, ever since Ma had died.

But in a way to Constance, Ma had died the day Samuel left. When her only son never returned she became a shadow of a woman, and clung on to her daughter with a peculiar mixture of desperation and hatred, apparently resenting that it was Constance that remained. Constance always supposed that Ma would have preferred if it had been her that had disappeared and not her brother. But Constance was all she had, so Ma kept her close, fearful that she too would disappear.

Constance always wondered why she didn't, why she felt undeserved loyalty to remain. Perhaps she supposed that Samuel would return and she wanted to be there when he did.

Then Ma got ill. Cancer, that's what the doctor had said, terminal. He offered treatment to make the remaining months a little more bearable, but Ma refused to leave the farm. In the days when she was delirious with pain she wouldn't recognise her daughter. She'd yell out for her husband, for her boy. It always came down to Samuel in the end. There would be accusations made against the very daughter that changed her sheets and got her on the potty. How Constance would never leave him be, and it was her fault he went, because she heard the raised voices in the barn. Her useless daughter had driven her boy away, because of what she was and what she had done. It was the shame.

After one particularly bad night Constance had walked out of the bedroom and had escaped outside. It had been a balmy night, the height of summer, and the air was still tinged with the heat of the sun. When she had gone back Ma was on the floor. Her body unnaturally twisted and still, her eyes open and glassy, staring up at the door. Constance knew it was Samuel she waited to walk through it and not her.

'And who is this handsome chap? Some old boyfriend eh?' William had picked up the frame with the photograph of Samuel. It was one of those official ones. He was wearing his uniform and was smiling, though it was a forced expression. Constance could see the fear in his eyes, like a child on its first day at school. She remembered the day he had returned, and she had held him for hours in her arms, her lips still wet from his kisses. 'One that got away eh?' William shook his head and put the frame back on the mantelpiece.

It was wrong what they did, her and Samuel. Constance knew that. But all they had was one another. When Pa died it seemed her world fell apart, and then Samuel was there, to pick up those pieces, to put them together and make her feel whole again. They weren't even sure what they were doing the first time. What they knew they learnt from the animals around them, and it came as natural as breathing. Constance soon came to crave those moments when the pair of them lay in the barn, limbs entwined. It was always them both against the world. Next to Pa, Samuel was the only man Constance had ever loved and would ever love.

'It's my brother actually,' Constance hissed, the words stinging her tongue.

V

William stared at the photograph, and then looked at her with such intensity that Constance squirmed.

'I can see the family resemblance now. It's the nose,' he said, touching his own, and smiling like a child might do. 'And this brother, where is he?' He was looking at her again.

Constance turned shamefully away, as if William were to stare into her eyes long enough he would be able to see the secret that all these years she had clutched onto possessively, like a child with a sweet snatched from a sibling's hand. 'He went a long time ago,' she said. She watched William's face fall a little, as he knew he'd said the wrong thing.

'You were close?' he asked.

Constance nodded, still not having the courage to look at him. 'Yes, we were, especially after Pa died.'

It had been a bad winter that year. There had been no weathermen to warn them, but Father had said it was a sign that the holly bushes were heavy with berries. He pointed out the abundance of them on one of their walks, and she had marvelled at the tiny bright red pearls that looked like jewels among the green of the holly. When the snow finally did come down it was heavy and settled quickly, a thick blanket which grew denser as the hours passed, and was so white it hurt your eyes to stare at it for too long.

It had always been a tradition of Pa's to give her a lamb in the spring. Of course, the young Constance hadn't realised that those thick hot slabs of meat on her plate on a Sunday were Daisy or Buttercup. Her father, as always, hid such an ugly truth from her. One of lambs survived, though, a sickly little thing that Pa thought wouldn't live its first month, but had defied his canny knack of knowing and missed the market. The snow was falling heavily by the time her father trampled back. Pa had only just begun to tug off his boots when she had tearfully begged him to go out and bring her sheep to her, though Ma had warned her that she wouldn't have any of the livestock in the house. Perhaps a stronger man would have told her not to be so silly, but Pa would have done anything for Constance. So he went out again. She remembered watching him, struggling against the arrows of snow, eventually becoming an insignificant blot of muddy colour that eventually became swallowed up by the fairy tale white.

It was last time Constance saw him alive.

They found Pa in the end, but had to wait until the snow stopped falling and settled thick like a layer of marzipan, before they could bring him back to the farm. She watched secretly from the window as they carried his body to the barn, stiff as a plank of wood, Ma trailing behind them, hunched up like a wounded animal. When she came back, her eyes hollow and lips trembling, Ma wouldn't allow Constance or Samuel to see him, but Constance was determined, wanting desperately to see her beloved Pa one more time, and a bit of her didn't quite believe that he was dead.

Constance had crept in and found him curled up on the straw. It was as if he was asleep, but there was something unnatural about the way his limbs were twisted around his body, as if he had tried to keep himself warm from the falling snow. His head nestled deep into his folded arms, just like a young Samuel trying to hide from the monsters he imagined creeping out from under his bed. Pa still wore his cap and this had bought a smile to her lips, though it was tinged with a kind of sadness. He looked sodden too and so she wrapped an old blanket around his wet shoulders, though it was too late for him to benefit from it. Constance hated the thought that he'd been out there alone, and she had laid next to him, her arm resting on his back. The cold of his body seemed to cling to her and for a few hours afterwards; she couldn't get warm.

Samuel had questioned her that night. He was curious, a typical boy keen to hear the gory details - perhaps a description of a face haunted by fear, or something more fitting for a hero, eyes staring up looking death full on. Constance had lied a little to her brother. She did not admit that Pa had hidden himself away, his eyes tightly shut, weak and afraid. Samuel had such a high opinion of Pa that she hadn't the heart to destroy it. And the image she relayed to him, Constance was convinced, Samuel carried inside from that moment onwards, and it began to shape the man that had emerged from the chrysalis of sorrow of that day.

They had been side by side in bed, their voices low so not to disturb Ma, who was finally sleeping after hours of sobbing that had radiated through the walls and had kept the pair of them awake. They had not shared a bed since they were babies, but that night they slept together, both eagerly wanting the warmth, as the house seemed a colder place without their Pa.

And there was another change in Samuel. The boy disappeared. There were no more childish games. Even Ma saw the transformation, and she, without difficulty, accepted his new role. However, she showed nothing but resentment to her daughter. Constance suspected she may have been a bit jealous of the close bond she and her brother shared. The same jealously that had gripped Ma the moment she had been born and Pa had taken her up into his arms and had held her close to him preciously.

'You miss him still?' It seemed more like a statement than a question. It was as if William had read her thoughts.

'Every day I think of him, so yes.' Constance pursed her lips, hoping that those tears, which always seemed to threaten, would not fall.

'I'm so sorry. I've upset you, it's so hard isn't it, when people leave?' William looked wistfully past her, his meaningful stare implying that he was looking so much further than the hallway beyond.

'Have you lost someone?' Constance nervously studied

the man in front of her and saw how his jaw tightened, the soft kind mouth becoming hard and angular. He didn't answer, and it was Constance's turn to realise she had entered a territory of private grief. 'Samuel wasn't just my brother, he was my everything.' Constance continued, despite herself. She had looked away briefly and suddenly felt William's arm on hers. It was a soft but firm grip, the sort Samuel would give her when Constance doubted herself. She looked up, and was almost taken aback to see that it was William who was standing there and not her brother.

'I think we both need a cup of strong tea. Could you do that Constance, make us both one?' William still gripped her arm; his hand was tight now, and Constance wondered if he was trying to steady her as she felt a little light-headed and had begun to sway. 'Could you do that for me Constance?' William repeated his request. She nodded obediently, and he lessened his grip.

VI

Constance had rubbed at her arm, and when she had pulled back the sleeve of her jumper she found that the skin was red and smarting. The trembling she had attributed to the cold she felt now had become a violent shaking and she had to stand for a little while, trying to compose herself.

She began opening every cupboard. Eventually finding, in the last but one, the floral patterned cups and saucers that Ma would keep for best. She took two out, placing the cups tentatively down, fearing that the shaking of her hand would break them both. The last time they had been used was the day of Pa's funeral. The few relatives that were prepared to make the journey had stood in the living room, feeling out of place and uncomfortable in their Sunday best. Sam and Constance had stood in the corner, squirming under the pitying spotlight forced upon them. She remembered how she felt Sam's hand suddenly grip her own, his fingers entwining around each of her digits. Constance fought with the smile that began to take hold of her lips; even now she felt it with the memory of those hesitant finger tips. It was a moment of warmth on that day, when the coldness had begun to pour into every space of the house and never left it.

But if the unusual noise of strangers was unsettling to the two siblings, the heavy silence which followed it was much worse. Once the house was cleared, the best china returned to its resting place, Ma removed the polite smile she wore for the occasion. The mouth became hard, like a line slit into a piece of fabric. It became painful for Constance or Samuel to see the anxious twitch Ma gave every time Pa was mentioned. So in the end the pair spoke about him in whispers, huddled together under blankets.

That is how it began. That first kiss, faltering and unsure. Samuel testing himself, he had pulled back, his eyes wide and fearful of the consequences. But Constance had stared into those blue eyes, saw a little of her Pa, and had placed her lips back on his.

In the days after this kiss Constance would watch Ma with a nervy trepidation. Fearful that every twitch of her body when her brother's name was mentioned, an absentminded smile, or Sam and her crossing paths in the hallway with their bodies pressed close to one another would give the game away.

But if Ma noticed these little changes she never said or gave Constance any indication that she knew that such ungodly behaviour was occurring under her roof.

A small part of Constance knew it was wrong. Samuel

was her brother. But Constance was unable to stop herself. Even now her old body, most days tired and aching, trembled to recall the feelings she experienced. Constance swung so fast from each emotion she was never quite sure whether she was happy or sad. Most days she was in some no man's land, that precarious bit in the middle on which she teetered.

Constance bought the tray in. She had overfilled the teapot and, as she walked, tea escaped from its ill-fitting lid and dripped down the sides. William was perched on the edge of the chair.

'I hope you don't mind your tea strong. I've not got much milk,' she said.

William continued to ignore her, staring up at the mantelpiece. It had been some years since Constance had studied the photographs, which were lined up there, snippets of her family history now frozen in time. Ma and Pa on their wedding day, Pa smiling broadly, proud and happy with his lot, Ma only just turned sixteen looking less certain. Constance supposed that the young girl was nervous of what lie ahead as a farmer's wife. Perhaps, once upon a time she had envisaged an altogether different future for herself. There was even one of a younger Constance, coming gradually of age, certainly no child but not quite the woman that she became in the following year. She smiled at it, feeling more than a little sorry for the girl in the picture and the future that she was ignorant about. Then Samuel. The one that William had picked up, but there were others too. A baby bouncing on Ma's knee. She suddenly realised how happy Ma had looked, her hands holding tightly on to the small chubby body as if she feared he may escape from her. A boy with a mop of blond curly hair, though in black and white. She recalled how it was made even blonder by the sun, in a summer that was so hot the fields turned brown and dusty like sand, and Pa had been fearful that nothing would ever grow on them again. Constance wished that she could tell her younger self to appreciate those days. Those afternoons, which seem to stretch forever, walking through fields of ripening corn that itched at your legs. The wet autumns, feet sticking in mud, her Pa moaning and swearing as the rain seemed to always find an opening in his tightly buttoned coat and trickle uncomfortably down. They were happy days, in which innocence ran through every precious moment.

William spoke. 'So many memories, it must be nice to have a past, something you can escape to when things get rough.' He looked wistfully at the mantelpiece.

Constance had laid the tea things on a nearby table, and they balanced unstably on an underlay of old newspapers. 'How about your family?' She supposed he was married. Constance drew up a picture in her head, a young woman, with a child perhaps, in a smart modern little house, like the ones that had begun to spring up on the edge of her fields.

'I would have liked a brother. I was an only child, you see.' There was an edge of bitterness to his voice, as if he resented the fact that he had never been given the choice. 'Someone there... when things go wrong. I suppose you don't feel so alone do you?' William stared at her now, his voice imploring her to give some kind of answer, but Constance merely smiled with more than a little sorrow. It was true when Pa had died she and Samuel had clung to one another. But he had not been there when she had the child. There was only Ma to greet her when she had left it there. Ma with her hungry and desperate eyes, glad that she had come back and yet there was that edge of disappointment that, as the years went by, she was unable to disguise.

'But what about your parents? Are they still alive?' Constance bit her lip, studying William's face, trying to see whether she had said the wrong thing.

'My parents? Oh that is another story entirely.' William reached over and without asking began to pour, filling both teacups.

VII

William gripped his cup with both hands.

'Is it strong enough for you?' Constance looked eagerly, but could see that William's mind was on something other than the tea.

'I was adopted.' He stared at her, as if waiting for her reaction to this revelation. Constance merely nodded her head. She wasn't sure how he expected her to react and was nervous about making the wrong choice. 'A baby, they had me from a baby, so I haven't got any memories of my birth parents, not that they could give me much information about them.' He snorted, shook his head and pulled his lips tightly together, as if he was trying to prevent himself saying something else.

'They? You mean the authorities?' Constance was now sitting in the opposite chair, and had taken her own cup, though she hadn't touched a drop.

'Them, the pair that adopted me.' William spat this out with such venom that Constance jolted back quickly, and spilt some of her tea in the process. She winced as the hot liquid seeped through her skirt and burnt the skin of her thigh beneath.

'Perhaps they just didn't know, or didn't want to see you hurt?' Constance looked nervously at her visitor. He was on the edge of his seat now. She could see the tea cup trembling in his hand.

'It's pride. They didn't want to let me go; it would be a sign that they failed, you see.' William had grasped the handle of his cup so tightly that it suddenly snapped in his hand, and the cup, along with its contents, fell to the floor and lay in a puddle at his feet. He didn't appear to notice, or care. 'They were told they couldn't have a child. That's why they got me.' Constance was by his feet now, picking up pieces of the broken cup in her hand, and was laying them mournfully on the table. 'He tried his best, my so called father, pathetic sod.' He spat out the last word. 'But her...' He made another one of those peculiar wheezy puffs that he had started making, like he was about to laugh but suddenly changed his mind and was attempting to make it something else. 'I was a constant reminder, you see, that she failed.' William seemed sad for a moment, then leant back and Constance hoped that the anger, which had threatened to bubble over, now was abated. But it was a temporary reprieve because he soon sprang forward. 'I mean it wasn't my fault, was it? I didn't ask to be abandoned like that, discarded like a piece of crap. They didn't have to take me in, did they?' William glared up at Constance, and she wondered if he wanted some kind of answer.

Constance thought of her own dead boy.

'How about your mother?' Constance had taken a piece of the broken cup in her hand, and now was pressing the sharp edges against the tips of her fingers.

'Which one?' Again William made that snort, a laugh with no warmth or good humour behind it.

'The woman that gave birth to you, she may have had her reasons to let you go?' William shot her such a look that Constance pushed herself further back into the chair. His expression frightened her. She recognised it, the way the eyes narrowed, the jaw tense, his hands that were now scrunched up into fists. Samuel had been like that when she had told him about the baby. As if it was purely her fault.

'I would love to meet her, Christ yes.' He spat this comment out with bitterness.

Constance wondered what would have happened if her child had lived. Would it have resented being here on the farm, despising her, hating the father that had abandoned them both? Though it twisted her insides to think such a thought, she was almost glad that the child had died.

'I suppose I didn't help, though,' William continued, shaking his head as he spoke. 'Getting into trouble. School couldn't cope; they kicked me out in the end. Didn't know how to...' William's words petered out. He continued shaking his head. Constance could see a shadow of regret, taking a bit of the heat of his anger.

'It was your way of coping I suppose.' She thought about Samuel. The day he had walked away from her with such determination, as if he had a destination in mind. She had thought to herself, he'll be back, once he has calmed down. Perhaps disappearing like that was his way, abandoning her, and their child. Constance had wished he had lost his temper like William, even hit her if that is what it took to make him stay.

'I'll never forgive her, though.' He looked her squarely in her eyes and Constance knew who he was referring to.

'She probably had her reasons.' Constance shifted uncomfortably. She wondered if she had given herself away, and bit her lip with a fretful anticipation.

'What reason is there to abandon a child? You know what, my so-called father said that's what happened. I was just left to bloody rot. He said I was lucky he came that day.' William had twisted his hands into fists. Constance suddenly became frightened, and got up so sharply that she almost stumbled and was almost knocked over by William's flailing arms. 'I just can't get my head around it, why somebody would just give up on a child.' He shook his head as if he was trying to find some kind of answer but was failing dismally.

'Perhaps there were circumstances, circumstances out of her control.'

William looked at her then, that mouth pulled so tight, just like Samuel's had been on that day.

'What would you do with a baby?'

Constance looked up. It was the last thing that Samuel had said to her before he had walked away. And just like on that day, the question hung in the air, an accusation that Constance was unable to defend herself against.

VIII

'What would you do with a baby?' Samuel repeated it. The anger had lessened, but the look he gave her was much worse, as if she didn't deserve such a thing, that she was incapable.

Of course, Ma was going to find out about the baby; Constance could not hide it forever. She had walked in on Constance, who was attempting to swaddle her now swollen belly with layers of skirt. Ma had stood still, unable to speak, looking at her daughter with a kind of disbelief. Unsure, perhaps within that moment, of what emotion to choose. And then she made her choice very clear when she spat out the word 'whore', grabbing Constance so tightly by the arms that huge welts blushed the surface of the skin, remaining there for some days after. Ma shook her so violently that Constance feared for the baby and held her belly tight. She dared not look into Ma's eyes, supposing they would reach into Constance's very heart and read the name that had made its mark there.

Ma had told her about the woman in the village. Unmarried and with no children of her own, there were always rumours, usually from the women, and she imagined Ma among them, picking up what titbits she could. Some of the villagers even hinted at a darker past of witchcraft, but Constance had only seen a lonely woman who curried favour by doing what she could to gain a bit of human warmth. Ma had said this woman would get rid of the baby. It was well known that if nature wasn't wanted to take its course, then old Mary could finish the job. Constance had shaken her head. It was her and Samuel's, no matter how wrong. Constance had seen the child like an unexpected gift. Ma was angry. She even threatened to throw her daughter out; although, Constance wondered if Ma could ever do such a thing. Since Pa had died, Ma had kept her son and daughter close, treating them like possessions that she owned and with no intention of letting them go into the world and away from the farm. Though Samuel was her prize, her daughter had her uses too.

Constance had hoped of a secret weapon in the form of Samuel. That whatever Ma thought, Samuel would not want to kill the child. Their child.

She chose her moment carefully and spoke with Samuel outside the house. It had been several days after the argument with Ma, who had watched her every move. Samuel had looked at her apparently wide-eyed and disbelieving when she had told him.

'A baby?' Samuel had stepped away, and Constance attempted to hold him, desperate to keep him close, as if the separation would break the thread she believed bound them close. He spoke about the child then as if it were hers alone and he played no part in its conception. Constance supposed that in his head he imagined some other man, a separate person who had defiled his sister. This idea was like a parasite, eating away at her insides, gnawing so at each muscle and attached sinew that she thought she might collapse. She watched him cautiously as he paced around the barn, biting the skin around his nails. He stared at her wide-eyed again when she mentioned Ma's plan, the woman in the village, but then nodded his head. Samuel took her by the shoulders, but it was not a gesture of love, not the way he had held her in their moments alone, his hands gently pressing into her skin, his fingers caressing through the fabric of her clothes, lovers in gentle cohesion on whatever was their bed. This time those same hands, now as red and rough as Pa's had been, gripped her flesh and hurt. He hissed over and over again that she must get rid of it. Constance had hated those words, spoken like it was a cancerous lump that had no rightful place in her body, a foreign piece of matter that could be cut out and discarded. But to her, the baby was a fruitful conclusion to their love. She couldn't understand how anybody, especially Samuel, could not see that.

When Constance had walked away back to the house she saw Ma in one of the windows, her arms folded, her face set in grim determination. She knew then Samuel's surprise had been feigned, that Ma had already told him. She had hoped her son would talk some sense into his sister. Samuel's initial disbelief had begun from the moment he had left the house. It was as if he had cleared away the time he and Constance had spent together, and in its place was a horrible dirty lie. Pa had always loved her, nothing could stop him even when Ma had scolded him for spoiling her. He would try his best to look stern, but out of Ma's steely iron glare he would pinch her cheek mischievously, then grin like he was a child himself and the two of them were sharing a secret.

But Samuel was very much his mother's son.

Constance had remembered her brother's eyes; it was as if their bright blue had been washed away, replaced by two impenetrable circles of black. It wouldn't have mattered how hard she pleaded, he wouldn't have seen the fear she had within her own eyes. He would have failed to see her love for him, like he failed to pay any mind to the single tear than ran down over the contour of her cheek.

'You're crying.' William's hand came up, a finger lightly touched the solitary tear and let it drop, studying it for a while. Constance fought the urge to grab his hand, to pull it back to her cheek, but suddenly felt ashamed. He would feel the wrinkled skin of an old woman, skin that had braved thirty or more years of harsh winds and bright sunshine since her Samuel had left. It would repulse him, and at this moment she didn't want that. She was happy in the warmth he was now showing.

'I miss him so much.' William held her now. Those arms supporting her.

'Samuel?' William whispered. He was so close to her now. She resisted the urge to collapse completely into his embrace. If she closed her eyes, it would be her Samuel that would be in front of her. Constance could smell him, that earthy scent, a lifetime spent on the fields and in the open air. Her Pa smelt the same. It was ingrained and couldn't be washed away.

'My baby. I miss my boy.' Constance let herself slide down.

IX

'You had a child?' William was knelt down beside her.

40

The hands, which had prevented her from sprawling at his feet, now seemed to tighten their grip. He was lifting her up, pulling Constance towards him, wanting an answer.

'Yes... yes my baby...,' Constance spluttered out in between desperate sobs and gasps of air. She had held it in for so long. Whilst Ma was downstairs she pushed her face into her pillow, eventually she learnt to cry without any sound at all. The longing for the child, for Samuel, buried itself deep inside. Her grief became as natural as breathing itself.

'You have to tell me who the father was. Who was he?' William hissed. Constance turned her head away.

'He left us. He left us both.' She could not contain the sobs now. Her body shook, and it seemed it was William that was the only physical thing that kept her from floor beneath.

'And the child? What happened to the child?' William's face was close. She could feel his breath on her cheek, but she was still afraid to look at him.

'He was dead. I tried... tried to revive the poor little thing, but he was dead.' Constance now could see the baby. So still and cold to touch. She had never wished for anything so hard in her life, perhaps that Pa would come back to her, but on that day she wished only that the child would live.

'Was it dead Constance really? Or did you panic?' William's voice was softer now. The grip on her arms, though still as secure as before, had softened too a little and it felt more like he was trying to hold her.

'No!' she yelled out with an unexpected anger, and this time stared at him, her eyes blazing. 'I tried, but the little thing was cold, so cold.'

William let go. Constance felt herself fall to her knees, and was rocking to and fro, wrapping her arms around herself as if the child was within them and she was soothing it to sleep.

She had wanted to hold him when she had returned. On the slow walk across the field Constance played the scenario in her head, a final goodbye before laying her baby forever within the cold soil.

'It was not there. It was not there,' Constance wheezed between painful cries. She had searched, though it was dark. Eventually she had to return to the farmhouse. That night Constance lay in her bed unable to sleep. Every time she closed her eyes she would see that little body, shrivelled up. Not that it would be any warmer buried, but there was something final to that, rather than the child just being left to the elements. When eventually she gave up on the idea of sleep, she pressed her face against the window pane, hoping that some deeper instinct would guide her to the spot.

Constance returned to the field, glad to get away from Ma's prying eyes, which seemed to follow her about the kitchen. She searched and searched, and only gave up when she recognised her footprints on the ground she had already explored.

'I couldn't understand where it had gone. I searched so many times.' And Constance did, visiting the supposed spot each year and standing there, as if somehow, like some kind of seed, the child had buried itself deep into the earth and would sprout up, a shoot of new life.

The sound of something shattering brought Constance back into the room. At her feet was the photo frame with the picture of Samuel. The photograph still remained in the frame, but the ochre tinted surface now glittered with shards of broken glass.

Constance felt William's hand on the back of her neck. He was pressing hard, forcing her head down and her body followed obediently. William was pushing her face determinedly into the broken pieces. Constance squeezed her eyes shut, frightened that some of the tinnier slithers would blind her. She felt his breath on her ear. Some curls of William's hair must have escaped from his otherwise combed back fringe and tickled her cheekbone.

'So you just left me there to rot, did you? Hoping that I would die in the cold?'

Constance cowered. He had to understand, it was never like that.

'I tried, but you weren't breathing.' Constance began to shiver herself. She opened her eyes and realised that the fire had gone out, and the chill, which had crept steadily in, now consumed the whole room.

The cold. It had always been here. When the baby died, when Samuel had left. Perhaps it began when Pa died. Slowly, so gradual that she never quite realised until now, and it gripped her without letting go.

'Please William, I thought you were dead. The baby was dead when I left it there. I went back. I couldn't find him.' He was on top of her now; she had the lapel of his jacket in her clenched fists. But she did not want to fight him. Her boy, he had returned to her and in this moment, awful that it was, she didn't want to let him go.

Constance could feel William pulling at her skirt. She heard something ripping, and took a sharp intake of breath as the air stung her naked thigh. Constance quickly realised his intentions now. Her hands began to claw at him. She yelled out. She didn't know why because there was no one to hear it, but it was a release, and she closed her eyes, hoping that the darkness would take her. How she would feel on those long winter nights when Pa had eased himself on top of her. She knew he loved her, though it wasn't the right way to show it. She hoped that her son would love her too.

William's lips were close to her. She suddenly felt his cold skin caress her earlobe.

'Inside, I want to be inside.'

Then she felt his hands on her thighs, forcing them apart. Constance tried to fight him at first, did her best to kick, and then her hands began to flail, pulling at his hair in desperation.

'I want to go back Mummy, back to where it's warm, back to where I belong.'

She continued to fight, but there was such a horrible inevitability to it all that in the end she gave up, let her limbs flop listlessly. She gasped as she felt his fingers push through the coarse thinning hair, pushing away the thin, wrinkled lips of her labia. The fingers intent and determined to continue their hellish journey, though she hissed and spluttered in pain. The agony consumed her, and there appeared to be no end to it, just as it was on the day her son was born.

Outside the snow, which the weatherman had promised, now fell. Large, almost weightless flakes that settled on the ground below. And, after a few more hours, it covered the fields, and the farmhouse within them, in a shroud of white.

X

Graham had been out all day, leaving Margaret still in bed. But often it was like that, and if he had finally realised that she was only pretending to be asleep, he had not let on. Whilst curled up foetus position, the duvet wrapped around her possessively like a second skin, Margaret would hear him move around the room. Graham was quiet. Anybody else would not have been disturbed, but she had lain awake since the early hours, hearing each sound, each tiny movement. Sometimes she even thought she could hear his heart beat, slow rhythmic thuds, and there were days where she longed for silence. Margaret listened to Graham creep, slide the drawer open and take out a pair of the socks that she had paired and laid in rows, one for each day of the week. The wardrobe door barely made a sound, but she heard that slight creek and imagined him staring into its interior, studying each pair of trousers, every shirt. Sometimes Margaret would smile. Like he had a choice. Each shirt the same, identical trousers, she could take out an outfit with her eyes blindfolded and come out with something he had taken half an hour to decide on. She waited until she heard the front door. Of course, he was considerate enough not to bang it shut.

Graham was always considerate.

Margaret then moved listlessly out of bed and sat there for a while, staring down at her feet. She was building herself up, preparing herself to stand. Sometimes it took a few minutes; other times she could be like that for hours, until the desperate urge to go to the toilet gripped her. Then Margaret would walk with clumsy steps to the bathroom, eventually climb into the shower and let the hot water fall over her. Afterwards she always felt a little better. It was just those moments before that took such a while.

Margaret wondered how long she had been like this. Sometimes a photo in one of the frames downstairs would catch her eye. A woman that seemingly looked like her, smiling. She touched her own mouth and tried to lift the corners up, but it just didn't feel right.

She must have been happy once. Sometimes Graham would talk about their wedding. What a wonderful day it was. How it'd been raining cats and dogs for weeks, but that day, that day the sun had shone and it almost felt warm. How that unexpected sunlight had bought out the best in everyone. When he talked Margaret tried to remember the day herself, but all she could picture was a child of a cousin crying throughout the ceremony, huge painful sobs that echoed around the church. In the end the child was taken outside, soothed by its mother and squares of chocolate.

He struggled at times, found it hard to keep up the pretence of being the good patient husband. It would start with the hushed, secretive phone calls to his sister, who used to visit, but she hadn't been for months. Sometimes Graham would come home from work later than normal, a little drunk. Margaret would listen with a fearful anxiety as he climbed the stairs, stumbling always on that final step. His hand would reach out to her when he finally collapsed on the bed, but she would remain huddled into a ball, her hands pulled into fists. Graham knew it was pointless pursuing it any further, so eventually would turn over. She would listen, relaxing finally on hearing the steady in and outtakes of his breath in sleep.

Margaret had been on the sofa when he had returned. Hearing the key turn slowly in the front door she switched the television off. She still felt a little ashamed that she sat there every day staring at it. Graham was carrying something, a bundle, and she suddenly realised that within the fabric something was moving.

'What have you got there?' She was curious enough to get up off the sofa. He was holding it possessively at first, as if he were afraid of her reaction, but there was a smile too, creeping around the edge of his lips.

'It's for you, us.' Graham held it out then, his present. She peered down and almost gasped to see the small, pale face of a baby staring up at her.

They were told at the hospital that the likelihood of them having children was non-existent. She recalled that empty feeling in the consulting room, the expression the doctor had given Margaret when he had shaken her hand. In the car Graham had held her hand, his other stroking her shoulder, trying to persuade it and the rest of her body to rest into his, but she was rigid. She wanted desperately to be alone.

'We could adopt you know. It would still be our baby,' he had said to her at a later date, with that pitying tone in his voice that made her feel nauseous. He tried to say it like he believed it.

Graham had laid the child next to her, and she had pulled back the shawl it had been wrapped in. The white pathetic little body still bloody from its mother.

'You haven't...?' Margaret couldn't really believe he would do such a thing. He caught on quickly and shook his head, his eyes wide with horror, hurt that she actually supposed that the man she had been with for over ten years was capable of such awful crime.

'God no, Margaret, no. I found it, really, just lying there, poor little mite had been abandoned. If I hadn't, well if I hadn't been there, it would have died, frozen to death.' He shook his head and shivered as if imagining this. Graham knelt down then, his huge hands stroking the child's face, and it pursed its lips, its eyes suddenly snapping wide open, responding to this human touch, looking up at the man who had just saved its life. Graham had smiled then. The first real smile for months. It lit his face up, and for the first time in such a long while Margaret felt something hopeful stir inside, and she took this as a good omen.

When Graham had gone to work the next day she had watched the child for a while. It seemed to have more colour today. That warm pinkish hue, its tiny chest rising up and down, a picture of contentment. In the night she had awoken from a strange dream, and had slowly made her way to the spare room where they had made up a bed for the baby. Margaret had peered down and found to her horror that the child was pale, and when she knelt down and stretched out her hand, tracing its cheek with her finger tip, it was so cold it made her shiver. She supposed the child was dead, and she rocked back and forth for a while, wondering if she should tell him. What would they do with a dead baby? How could they explain it? Margaret felt bile rise up and hit the back of her throat. She bent further down, her ear close to his mouth and still heard nothing at all.

'What is wrong?' Graham's voice suddenly from the doorway.

In the semi-darkness she envisaged the concerned expression on his face. He was by her side suddenly, pushing her gently out of the way, perhaps he didn't quite trust her yet.

'He's fine,' he said. There was an element of surprise in his voice. Margaret looked down now. It was moving, small twitches of its body, gradually coming back to life. 'That's my boy eh? You're fine aren't you William?' She hadn't realised he had named the child.

Lying there in the darkness, Margaret wondered if she had imagined that the baby was dead. There was a momentary unease that perhaps, deep down, she wished it was.

Tell Me

If it hadn't been for the odd passer-by wrapped up like a North Pole explorer, Robert could have been almost deceived into thinking it was June rather than January. As he looked through the windscreen, the sky was bright blue and cloudless. The sun so bright he impulsively rifled through his glove compartment to find his sunglasses, which he had abandoned in there since last summer.

This was the seaside of his childhood. He'd spent many a summer holiday here, and no matter how many exotic holidays he had since, it was Coombe Bay that made him smile like he was a boy again. He could recall the journey down; in those days it was on the train, Mum, Dad, Angela and a variety of cases and bags, lugged through the station with much grunting and moaning.

But there was always this. All four of them standing on the edge of the beach, trying to resist the urge, if only for a few minutes, to pull off socks or stockings and bury their toes within the sand.

Robert wistfully believed he was standing on that same spot, and almost succumbed to a nostalgic whim to plunge naked feet into the sea as he once would, but that chilly breeze whipped around his neck, and as he pulled up the collar of his coat tighter, just like the idea of wearing his sunglasses, it was quickly dispelled.

However, he was unable to resist licking his lips and

tasting the salt that lay on the surface of them, and that unexplained boyish pleasure made him grin.

Robert listened contently to the hush of the waves. He was a man well past a need for bedtime stories, but it was his favourite lullaby when he couldn't sleep. A seagull cried overhead, and there was something sorrowful about the sound over the beach. Robert smiled. So typical of him to attach sentiment; the bird was probably moaning of the lack of rich pickings, as now only the dog walkers and the broken-hearted frequented the bay at this time of the year.

When the chill of the air had crept further in Robert began to walk briskly. He still felt cheery despite the cold. Many would have thought the beach looked desolate and empty, or feel the absence of the trill squeals of excited children, but Robert found a comforting solitude to the place, a tranquillity that life back at home just didn't allow. Not that he regretted his life in a busy market town and the social circle that went hand in hand in with living in the same place for twenty years, but he appreciated this quietness. It gave him time to do a bit of thinking, perhaps even to give a thought to that novel that he'd been itching to write for as long as he could remember.

Today though, he thought about his father. When his father had been alive the pair of them had come here at least once a month to follow the same path he was walking now. Even after the old man suffered a stroke they continued this monthly pilgrimage, with Robert pushing his father's heavy frame in a wheelchair. He had died five years ago, and Robert still missed him. In those later years they became more like friends, and Robert slowly got to know the man beneath the parent he had been bought up by. He quickly blinked away a tear. Arnold Gibson would have thought it a foolish for his son to waste emotion on a life that had been long, much longer than that of Robert's mother.

Robert had been so deep in thought that he almost stumbled into the man who was sat hunched over his knees, and who had looked up as Robert gave a girlish 'oh' of surprise. It was not the kind of weather to be sitting idly looking out to sea, but the man sat there as if this was one of those wonderful hot days in summer that takes you by surprise. The man was such an unusual sight. Robert, quite out of character, gave a quick nod of acknowledgment and walked swiftly by.

But Robert couldn't quite shake off the thought of that man sitting alone. An unexplained sense of guilt unexpectedly washed over him. It would be perfectly reasonable to assume the stranger wanted to be left undisturbed. The man had not really taken much note of Robert strolling along the seafront, but Robert had suddenly remembered how he was just after his father had died. Robert took to having long walks, often standing still as he was suddenly gripped by a memory, as one sometimes does when mourning some kind of loss. People had passed him by, too busy or perhaps assuming he had wanted to be alone. He had raised his head up to catch them looking awkwardly in his direction, and there had been this sudden longing for one of them to stop. A perfect stranger, with whom he could have spoken aloud of all the grief and fear that came along with losing that one remaining parent. The things he felt too awkward to say in front of his family, even his dear wife.

Robert made a promise to himself, that on the way back, if the man was still there he would at least stop. Even if the man didn't want to speak, it would ease his conscience, and it wouldn't play on his mind in the car on the way back home.

The man was indeed still there on Robert's return

journey, in exactly the same position, like one of those carved statues that were sold in the gift shops in the town during the summer months. And Robert, true to his word, stood by the hunched figure.

Apparently so deep in thought, the man didn't even sense that Robert was standing next to him and flinched when he began to speak.

'Look, I'm sorry to disturb you, but are you alright?' Robert gave the man one of his nervous smiles. His wife always nicknamed it his 'sorry grimace', as she said he always wore the expression when he'd done something wrong. 'I noticed you on my walk you see ...' Unusually for rather a confident man, he stumbled over his words. Robert pushed his hands into his pockets, and it was in the security of those dark crevices they were liberated to fidget nervously.

Robert was able to study the man a little more closely now he was standing over him. The face was pale, and a layer of thick black stubble made it look dirty and unkempt. The eyes seemed to retreat deeply into the sockets and underneath them there were dark circles, hinting that the man hadn't slept well for weeks. He appeared to have the weight of the world upon his shoulders and they were hunched under the strain.

The man looked up and said nothing.

Robert shuffled uncomfortably. Perhaps he should just leave the man alone. It was obvious that whatever was troubling him he wanted to deal with it by himself. Yet the man's eyes, there was something in those pools of grey that made Robert sit by his side.

'Do you mind? That walk has worn me out and the car is way up there,' Robert said, gesturing and catching a glimpse of his vehicle, realising that it was the only one parked there. The man shrugged his shoulders nonchalantly.

The cold of the concrete beneath him made Robert shiver a little. It seemed to penetrate through his heavy overcoat, and he suddenly yearned for the warmth of his car.

'I used to come here as a boy. My parents would bring me and my sister here every summer,' Robert continued after a pause to allow the man's reply that never came. It was strange, but he suddenly realised that he had not thought about his sister for a long while. Angela was only five years older than him, but she had taken the role as older sibling very seriously, and the young Robert was forever the brunt of her bossiness; but he always believed there had been affection behind it, a kind of motherly instinct that prepared her for the role when their mother died. It was a shame that she took that man's side, a great shame that, in the end, Angela had chosen her husband over the brother she had treated like a son at times.

'It must have been busier then ... the beach.' The man finally spoke and looked up, staring out thoughtfully for a moment or two, and then let his head drop down once more.

'Yes, on one of those rare hot days you can't move for people.' Robert looked out. It was difficult to imagine it now, that bare sand filled with holiday makers. The return of the seagull ahead and its sad calling did nothing to disperse the sense of emptiness.

'I much prefer it like this,' the man hissed, his chin still pressed against his chest.

'My wife always says I'm a good listener.' Robert couldn't help but smile to think of Julie. She was probably at home right now, on the phone as always. She liked to talk so, of course, the man she married had to learn to listen well.

'Have you ever had a secret?' The man turned and glared. Robert shook his head and looked away as the man's stare made him feel quite uncomfortable. Secrets, he had learnt by bitter experience, were like untreated wounds that eventually would fester and infect what was otherwise healthy. His own mother had known that, God rest her soul. 'I think about it every day, every hour, every minute ...' the man continued, gulping as if he was about to burst into tears, and Robert looked away uncomfortably. He was of the generation who believed men shouldn't show emotion. Thankfully, the man recomposed himself, but Robert nervously wondered if it was just a temporary reprieve.

'Perhaps it would do you some good if you told me. It can't be that bad, surely?' Robert nervously smiled. He was quite alone here; a while back he'd seen that man with his dog, but they had been walking in the opposite direction and were miles away by now.

'Why would you think that? Do I look like a bad person?' The man shot Robert an accusatory glance, and his expression appeared to suggest that he wanted an answer. There was an awkward silence.

'I don't know you, but no I don't think that.' Robert stared at the ground, fearful of looking into those empty eyes once more. 'So you can tell me.' Robert was curious, he couldn't quite help himself, and it annoyed him as much as the bit of him that had to keep his promise to himself.

'I can?' It was as if the man had never thought about it before. Robert wondered how long the man had been coming here, staring out at the sea.

'A problem shared is a problem halved. That's what my old Nan would say.' Robert gave an embarrassed snort. He didn't quite believe this worn out phrase, but it seemed to work, and after a few moments of contemplation the man sidled nearer to Robert until they were almost touching.

Robert felt the hot breath against his ear. The smell of his companion rose up, a peculiar concoction of musty fabric and perspiring skin that had been unwashed too long. His voice, a hushed whisper in Robert's ear, had an accent that he couldn't quite place, and which seemed to roam from Irish to the Midlands with each sentence.

Anybody passing by would have assumed that the two men were great friends, but if they had observed a little more keenly, given the scene a bit more time than a passing glance would allow, they would have spotted the steady unease emerging from Robert - how his shoulders, once relaxed now stiffened, hunched down as if supporting a great weight. Robert's hands, to begin with calmly rested on his knees, were now clasped tightly together as if in prayer, gripping so tightly that the skin had become white and almost bloodless around the knuckles. Robert had the kind of lips that a smile appeared to be the most natural of expressions on, but now they were set in thin, taunt lines.

The man too had changed since talking to Robert. In sharp contrast, he seemed to be sitting straighter with each sentence he whispered. The eyes, which had before stared towards the sea as though hypnotised, now darted behind to the road that led back to the car park.

When they had finally finished. The man leant back and let out a sigh. Robert, though, did not acknowledge it and remained staring ahead.

'You know I feel better, really it's like a weight's been lifted off me.' He smiled, though the lips were still not used to it, and appeared uncertain for a moment or two. He looked up, pulled the collar up tighter around his neck. 'Think I'm going to be heading back. It's cold, too cold to be sitting here.' He slapped Robert on the shoulder playfully before getting up.

Robert didn't notice he had gone, or acknowledge the wave of goodbye. He was staring at the sea, his head slumped, the neck disappearing into his collar. The tide was creeping in, and he was unable to take his eyes off the constant gentle lapping of the waves.

Even the seagull, who had been following him and had circled overhead whilst he had sat, screeched despairingly, as if to get his attention.

The Eye of the Beholder

He watched it with a kind of trepidation, though the most delicate bit was already done. He had never quite lost the thrill that he had discovered as a boy. Even now, in the darkness, he fingered the reel excitedly, like it was the first time all over again. One clumsy movement, the slightest chink of light and all that effort lost. Each time there was a feeling of expecting something miraculous. As if he were a magician, and the ears of that rabbit were tantalising close to his fingertips. That's what he had always thought of his grandfather, who had shared his secrets during one summer holiday. A wizard, creating spells, making beautiful pictures from trays of nothing.

She had sat nervously in the sitting room, looking out of place on that shabby sofa, among the newspapers and well-thumbed books. Her posture screamed out for an elegant drawing room in some manor house in the middle of nowhere. She didn't belong in the seedy flat of some photographer, whose daytime job consisted of passport photographs and pet portraits.

'I heard about you from a friend.' She had stumbled over her words, and he was not sure if she was telling the truth. But then did it matter how they found out? They came all the same, all with the same apprehension, hands wrung, lips bitten, worried half-hearted smiles. He always wished he could reassure them beforehand, but still, that was part of the enjoyment wasn't it, seeing their faces afterwards.

She was emerging. Gradually, blurred lines became sharper, a cheek, her chin. He stopped himself taking it out, a few more seconds, just to bring out those eyes. Then he retrieved it, shook it a little before holding it up.

She was beautiful.

Nick stared at the calendar. It was Thursday, 15th March 1979 already. It felt like the New Year celebrations had only been a couple of weeks ago, but the year was already two and a half months old, and what had he to show for it? There had been one decent splash recently, his piece on petty officialdom - 'Britain's worst little Hitlers', decent enough exposure, true, but it hadn't really been a story of his creation, just one hanging on the coattails of some other written by a colleague. What would he be doing next? Not following in someone else's footsteps again; his next story would be a serious one and his own. His ambition demanded it be so.

Andy Granger, his editor, had been quiet for a few minutes, looking down at the photographs and then back to the typed proposal. He was a stout man of fifty-six and there had been rumours that he was thinking about retiring. Andy could see himself in that chair, not quite filling it as well as his boss, but looking equally as at home in that soft black leather.

'Hmm interesting.' Andy was trying to look unimpressed, but the lips were struggling to conceal a smile, and that was always an indication that he liked the story.

'So, what do you think? Got to admit it I've got something.' Nick lent forward, his right eyebrow raised, trying his best to restrain his childlike enthusiasm. Andy was now studying the photographs that were spread out on his desk, occasionally picking one up, putting it down, like a player looking for a good hand.

'Got to admit it, these women are stunning. I wonder where he finds them, this Will Harper, eh?' Nick followed his boss's gaze. The women captured in every shot were beautiful - too perfect actually, like some mad scientist had taken the essence of what was deemed the ideal woman and had created these creatures in some sterile laboratory.

Nick had discovered the story quite by accident. He was in his usual haunt, The Beehive, which was in danger of becoming an overpriced pub now it had been discovered by a richer clientele. That night he was meeting an old college friend, who now was something of a hack on a down-market tabloid sheet, but had enough stories and sometimes a free line to keep Nick entertained for a few hours. But the guy had not turned up, so instead Nick had got talking to some man at the bar. The man didn't represent The Beehive's aspiring new clientele, he repaired washing machines. However, Nick's interest was piqued when the man suddenly starting talking about a house he had made a call to, which belonged to a photographer. The washing machine repair man was an ex-con, and a bit of him just couldn't resist creeping around the house. He found the photographs quite by accident, whilst rifling through a cupboard. He tried to convince Nick that he hoped to frame them and sell them on, but Nick suspected he probably had seedier designs on them. He had shown them to Nick with a boyish greed.

Nick had been struck right away, and had bought several more rounds before offering the man twenty quid for the lot - a sum the man accepted so greedily that Nick supposed he might have offered him less. He had also managed to get the address where the photographer lived. Nick didn't have any scruples about the photos technically being stolen property. He didn't care, and he and the man wouldn't see each other again. He knew that.

'I've got to admit it. I'm intrigued.' Andy licked his lips, and suddenly put his hand up to cover them, as if trying to hide an obvious desire that had unexpectedly given itself away. Nick saw his boss give a furtive glance at the photograph of his wife framed on his desk, then quickly turn his gaze back to Nick. 'So,' Andy continued, 'I will put myself out of a limb here and let you run with it. I want some kind of rough outline by Monday at the latest.' He had gathered the photographs up, but couldn't resist glancing over them again as he shuffled them in his hands. Nick did his best to conceal a confident smirk, but he didn't quite pull it off, and Andy's face darkened a little. 'And don't let me down. You've been lucky, but if you don't pull this one off, Nick, you'll be doing the horoscopes.'

Nick had rung the number scrawled on the back of one of the photographs, and only when a voice suddenly said hello at the other end did he realise he hadn't got any kind of story properly prepared. It was only when he began to turn the photographs over that he caught a name on the back of one of them.

'Ruth? Yes, of course I remember,' the voice on the other end said, and there was an awkward pause before the speaker continued. 'It was so unexpected. Sorry, were you a friend of hers?'

'Cousin. We hadn't seen each other in a while, I'm afraid.' One of the many lessons Nick had learnt in being a journalist was that a lie had to be said with confidence.

'Ah, yes I see. Ruth said that after the accident, well, she kind of lost touch with a lot of her family.'

'That's understandable.' Nick's brow furrowed a little. He had to be careful now. 'So you're a photographer? Were you and Ruth good friends?' There was hesitancy at the other end of the line, the man's breathing quickening.

'No... not exactly. She wanted me to take her photograph, you see I've gained a bit of reputation.' The man on the other end gave a nervous laugh.

It had been easy to gain Will Harper's confidence. The voice on the other end of the phone lacked a certain self-assurance. Nick always had a certain kind of charm. He found it easy to be everybody's friend, to use a certain amount of persuasion to get what he wanted. As the phone conversation had continued Will had unwittingly agreed to an afternoon meeting in his studio, and afterwards Nick could hear in his voice the disbelief that he'd been talked into offering such an invitation.

The so-called studio was in fact a rather small room in the photographer's dingy flat. The man who had opened the door was a rather plain, bespectacled thirty-something, whose handshake was limp and uninspiring. Will Harper appeared to be gripped with a certain awkwardness, which might have been endearing in some schoolboy, but in the man seemed almost pathetic. There was something friendly about the face, though, a trusting disposition that to an eager journalist like Nick was very useful indeed.

'Well it's great to meet you Will, really. Thanks for letting me come over like this.'

Nick was offered tea and shook his head, as he had passed a damp and chaotic galley kitchen on his way in that looked as if it hadn't been cleaned for weeks. The living room didn't look much better. Will had mumbled something about a break-in a week or two ago.

'I'm so sorry about Ruth. It must have been a shock. I mean, all what she went through with the cancer, but well, damn,' Will said in low, frightened tones. Nick gulped hard, covered his mouth instinctively to disguise any signs of nervousness, but Will read it as emotion. 'Christ I'm sorry man, really, but Ruth, she was amazing.' Will seemed to come alive then; his eyes lit up, and Nick recalled the beautiful woman staring out of that photograph and could understand the reaction.

'Yes, she was, lovely person. It's been a bit of a shock for all of her family,' Nick said. He was surely on safe ground with those statements, but he couldn't think how to follow them. They sat in an embarrassed silence for a few minutes, until Nick changed the subject and they began to talk about photography. 'Yeah, I did a bit at college.' Nick had spun some line about doing some foundation course in art and Will had enthusiastically revealed that he had done the same.

'Would you like to see my darkroom?' Will was grinning, like a schoolboy showing off his new bedroom to a friend.

'So this is where the magic happens, eh?' Nick said, trying to appear casual, but he was studying every inch of the room. It contrasted sharply with the flat. Everything in here was neat; there was nothing out of place. It was as sterile as an operating room.

'Oh, I just take the photographs, in the end it's them at the other end of the camera.' Nick couldn't quite put his finger on it, but he could sense it in the pit of his stomach. The journalist within had a nagging doubt that something was not quite what it seemed. He felt the nervous twitches begin at the corner of his mouth; his lips had questions on them, but he instead forced them into yet another smile.

'So, how do you get your subjects then?' Nick gave a chuckle, but he noticed how Will shifted uncomfortably.

'They come to me. Like I said, I've built up a reputation. They can trust me.' Nick's instinct was never wrong. There was something more here, a story other than some photographer taking photos of pretty girls. But then, the photograph caught his eye, and everything else didn't seem to matter anymore.

Nick had seen some beautiful women in his time. He even dated one several years ago, Swedish, couldn't speak a word of English, but it wasn't a desire for conversation that had drawn them together.

But the woman in the photograph. She was different. The eyes, they appeared to stare beyond the flat surface, come alive, bore into his. He gulped; his lips became dry and he wished he had not turned down the tea that was offered.

'That's my most recent, Gloria, a friend of Ruth's.' Will smiled proudly. He too stared at the photograph, but in his case it was more like a father proudly showing off his daughter. There was nothing sexual in his gaze, whereas Nick felt every nerve in his body quiver.

'Do you have her phone number?' Nick sniggered, trying his best to make a joke of his request, but there was a real need behind it that had steadily began to gnaw away at him. Will ignored Nick's laugh and took the question in all seriousness.

'I can't give you that, no way,' the photographer snarled, for him an atypical moment of anger, but it passed quickly like a shadow across his face. He then stared towards the floor, ashamed of this sudden outburst. 'I'm sorry, but it would be abusing the trust Gloria had in me to do that.'

Nick knew he wasn't going to get anywhere with his request, and a wave of disappointment washed over him. He wasn't used to it, and was forced to sit down. He let Will begin to explain about his techniques, how light played an important part in his work, whilst all the time Nick's eyes attempted not to strain at the photograph, at that beautiful woman that seemed so unattainable.

But Nick was not a man who accepted defeat easily. They had returned to the sitting room and the journalist within began to scan the room, some kind of address book perhaps, some more photographs with her number on the back. But the room was so cluttered that any logic he had tried to apply was lost in the mass of discarded books and magazines. Then his eyes settled on the tattered looking address wheel. Would Gloria's address and phone number be amongst the details recorded on its tattered cards? Nick decided it was worth trying to find out.

'That tea still on offer?' he asked, and Will Harper set off to make it for him. Will Harper trusted people. It couldn't be that easy, thought Nick; but it was. He didn't know Gloria's surname, but he found one and only one Gloria's address and phone number carefully recorded in the address wheel, before he heard Will returning on his way to the room. Nick pulled Gloria's card out from the wheel roughly, and had it in his pocket safely, well before Will's return with the tea. Nick stopped long enough to drink a few sips of it, before making his excuses and leaving, on the way out making a half-hearted promise that he would visit Will again.

By the time Nick had got to the address he was out of breath and flustered. He had run there with a speed that he thought he had lost long ago. Nick had stood outside the door for a moment to compose himself, and ran a shaking hand through his hair.

He couldn't see anything inside clearly as the door opened to reveal a corridor of darkness. The figure within it had stepped hesitantly back on seeing a perfect stranger standing there. Nick caught only the briefest of glimpses before Gloria hid herself behind the door.

'I'm sorry I thought you were...' Gloria let the sentence

trail out. 'What do you want?' Her voice was strained. There was a nervousness to the tone that hinted she might dissolve into tears at any moment.

'I'm sorry. I should introduce myself,' said Nick. 'I'm Ruth's cousin. I believe you knew her.' Nick smiled bashfully. There was a painful silence. 'The photographer, Will Harper, I kind of tricked him into giving me your address.'

Gloria stepped slowly into the light. Nick's face fell.

He knew he had stared too long. Gloria saw it too - her eyes quickly dropped to the floor.

'Look you better come in.' She ushered him in with a quick, frightened gesture, and Nick couldn't help but note the sigh that escaped as she closed the door behind her.

In the light of the living room he was able to see her properly. The eyes. The same beautiful eyes that had stared out from that photograph were staring at him now. But Nick found it hard to recognise much else from it. The mouth didn't quite form that easy smile in the flesh. It was the scarring, which pulled the left side of the face downwards, and so the lips appeared to follow suit, no matter what expression they attempted to convey. It was like someone was tugging the skin down with an invisible rope. Try as he might, he couldn't help but follow the thick coils of damaged skin, which ran like tramlines down the face and neck. He imagined these snakes of damaged skin continuing further down, and momentarily wondered, with a macabre fascination, where it eventually stopped.

'Ruth? You're family?' There was sternness in Gloria's voice, but Nick sensed the nerves behind it. He nodded, suddenly feeling a rare lack of confidence.

'I'm sorry. It is awful. Well, there are no words are there?' For the first time they stared directly at each other. Gloria bit her lip nervously.

'Can I ask you how...' Again Gloria's sentence trailed off without end. She continued, trying to turn her thoughts into words that made sense together, 'Will, for that matter. I don't mean to be rude, but it was him I was expecting. Ruth, well she was one of the first of his clients.'

'I found his details among Ruth's things.' Nick lied, daring himself to continue to look at Gloria. Those beautiful eyes were now on the edge of tears.

'Oh, you see, she never mentioned any family... strange nobody at all.' Those eyes searching him, Nick began to squirm, as if he were the oddity in the room.

'I just wanted to know about Will Harper, the photographs, well he showed me them.' He couldn't stall the question. There had to be a story; it just didn't make sense. 'Will, he didn't do that to you, did he?' Her eyes shot him a look of horror.

'Will Harper made me feel beautiful again. How could you think such a thing?' Her bottom lip trembled, but there was the sharp edge of anger to her tone. Nick could see the woman that possibly once was, and he mourned that they had never met before.

'I'm sorry, but well, this all seems a bit odd to me.' The journalist within him - his voice had lost its disguise, and he could tell that Gloria could hear it too.

'I think you ought to leave. I'm feeling quite tired.' Her hands formed fists, tense and white at the knuckles. She refused to look at him again.

Nick stared into his glass. The whisky, which had been in it, had helped steady his nerves and went some way towards soothing the disappointment that had washed over him. He wasn't used to not getting what he wanted. But the drink had done nothing to quell the feeling that there was still a story to be told - perhaps not the one that he had begun with, but something that was interesting all the same. Of course, it was a shame about the woman, and with the thought of her he licked his lips to get the taste of the whisky again. He grimaced. It was that photographer's fault. If only Will Harper had been straight with him at the beginning, he wouldn't have made such a fool of himself. Nick looked towards the bar. He'd have another one, to steady his temper if nothing else.

'I thought you would come back, Gloria called me,' Will sneered through a half-opened door. Gone was the welcoming smile, the kindness in the eyes. The face was darkened by mistrust that didn't suit that otherwise boyish face. The hands were tense and gripping the door as if his very life depended on not letting Nick in. Nick attempted a smile, but the air had mixed with the whisky and the facade he had so skilfully built up now crumbled away.

'Come on Will, what's really going on here?' Nick demanded. He leant on the wall, his hand on the door, knowing full well that only with the slightest push he could easily force his way in. But he didn't, instead enjoying the sensation of power it gave him, watching with a smile the way Will now appeared to creep nervously inward.

'I don't know who you are. Please just go away and leave me alone,' Will hissed, but he was still nervous and seemingly fighting away tears, like a boy who was cornered by the school bully.

'Oh come on Will. What's the story? I mean no amount of bloody lighting is going to transform that face,' Nick spat out, leaning unsteadily forward.

'There is no story. It's the attitude of people like you that brings them here.' The sudden anger in Will's voice took Nick by surprise, and he leant back clumsily, his legs almost buckling underneath him. 'It's what's inside, that's what I'm talking about. I wonder about you, eh? What would my camera see?' Will had taken temporary advantage and had opened the door that little bit wider. Nick saw a chance and pushed himself up, towering once more over the short and still nervous photographer.

'Perhaps you ought to show me then?' Nick pushed the door, almost knocking a surprised and unprepared Will to the floor.

Nick had woken with his bed sheets damp and coiled around his legs. His head was mussy, his mouth was dry, and there were the beginnings of the headache that was to come. He walked slowly and with his eyes half closed to the bathroom, where he splashed water onto his face and then the brown envelope caught his eye. It lay innocent enough on the bathroom floor. Nick suddenly recalled that he had thrown it there last night.

As he sat on the bed, the envelope now in his hands, Nick attempted to recall what happened. It came in bits, odd snippets that did not fit together. Will had taken his photograph. The memory of that bright flash made the dull ache of his head that bit sharper now. He remembered the passing of the envelope, a strange look on the photographer's face and trying to swallow the bile that suddenly rose up into his throat.

'My camera sees what's inside.' That's what Will had said. Nick turned the envelope over again in his hands. Eventually he held it still. This was stupid. It was just a photograph. But as Nick slowly began to tear it open, using unusually cautious movements, he realised that his hands were shaking.

Bricks and Mortar

Even after twenty minutes of leaning against a wall, Henryk could still not get his breath back, but at least his heart was returning to its steady beat and the pain that had gripped him so fervently had subsided enough for him not to think that he may be breathing his last. Imagine that. After all he had been through, to die on the street of something so ordinary as a heart attack. He had survived horrors beyond imagination, lived through near-starvation and not had his days ended by a bullet or poison gas. He smiled at the thought that that must make him one of the lucky ones; lucky hardly described the misery his life had been over the past few years.

How long had it been? When had he last climbed this hill? He didn't care to work it out, to recall all the destruction he had seen, all the chaos he had lived through. Another displaced person, along with so many thousands of others, trying to work out how to live in a country where it seemed almost everything had been destroyed and where, for a time, the most stable currency had been American cigarettes. It was different now, of course. They were talking of a *Wirtschaftswunder*, an economic miracle taking place. It had yet to reach him, though. He had lived the life of a transient over the past few years, finding work where he could, sometimes staying in one place for a long enough for it to begin to feel like home. But something inside him always tugged at him to move on. In recent months this something, this feeling, had only increased, and he accepted more consciously what he had known somewhere for a long time, that it was leading him back here. He looked down at his shoes, worn and overdue for replacement by months, if not years. His feet inside them were red and blistered and smarted. A superficial pain, unpleasant. Nothing compared to the pain that lived constantly inside him. Memories of the horror he had seen, memories which clawed at him and would replay themselves time and time again in his head when sleep evaded him, as it did most nights.

Henryk tried to recall a happier time when he had climbed this hill. He had been a fitter man, well-fed, healthy and people had smiled at him and were happy to wish him good morning. But before long he found himself fighting the train of the thoughts in his head. Before they led him to recall the long journey from occasional instances of being shunned, through the enactment of the laws denying him citizenship rights, to the ultimate classification of him, and all of his race, as *Lebensunwertes Leben*, life unworthy of life.

As he continued to rest against the wall, Henryk instead turned his thoughts towards studying the street he had once known so well. He could see it from here, the house. He knew it would still be standing, when so many homes had been reduced to rubble. It called to him, stronger now than ever before. And now he was so near.

Inge watched the man walking up the street from her window. She had woken up feeling strangely nervous, as if she had anticipated something bad was going to happen this day. As he got nearer her house she could see the man in clearer focus. He was dressed so shabbily, the clothes not seeming to fit. He was, she was sure, a Jew, and she tried to fight the feeling of revulsion. She continued to watch the man, unable despite herself to take her eyes off him, even when he stopped periodically to rest and catch his breath. As he restarted his journey after one such pause she eventually came to realise, to her horror, that he was heading towards her house. Inge clenched her jaw as the man took another pause and looked up in her direction.

Henryk hesitated. He had imagined this moment. The house and he together once more. It had spoken to him over the years; in his moments of greatest despair it had told him to carry on living, so that he could return. He could see an unfamiliar face at the window. It had not been alone all those years, then. A tear rolled down his cheek.

'Yes?' the woman sharply hissed at him. She had not opened the door fully, and her tense hand gripped it so that her arm seemed to bar his way. He studied what he could see of her through the gap she allowed. She was in her thirties, he supposed, an attractive woman, though her face carried too much make-up and her eyes seemed cold.

She was studying him too. The man in front of her held his head lowered like a child about to be told off. He looked pale, and in the few moments he'd been standing there he appeared to grow markedly more unsteady on his feet. Inge looked past him over his shoulder. She hoped that nobody had seen him approach the house. He hadn't replied to her, so she spoke again. 'What do you want? There is nothing here, nothing for you at all.'

He made no reply, but at that moment his remaining hold on his balance gave way. He fell forward then, eyes dazed and confused. Inge opened the door just in time, and suddenly found that she was supporting him upright. They stumbled backwards, and the pair had performed a strange little dance of balance and limbs before stumbling towards the stairs.

The man had leant on her as the pair regained their footing and she had found him to be surprisingly light. Unlike her late-husband, this man felt sharp and angular against her flesh. For a brief moment she had felt overwhelming pity for him, but now that he was sitting in the armchair that her husband had favoured, and seemed all too comfortable with it, her contempt for the stranger was returning. In her confusion of emotions and succumbing to a sense of politeness that her mother had done her best to instil in her, she had offered the stranger a glass of water, which he had accepted. She had been shaking as she handed the drink to him, a gentle but constant vibration that made the water in the glass shake. He sipped at it now and smiled uncomfortably at her.

Henryk was not quite sure what had happened. One minute he had been standing at the doorway, the next, a wave of clammy nausea had washed over him, unexpected and without warning. Henryk felt strangely happy to let himself go, and had welcomed the darkness like an old friend. But he had staggered towards the woman, he could remember that. And he had let himself be enveloped into her softness, the faint smell of cigarettes that mingled and strangely complemented the sweeter scent of her perfume. She now stood over him, and lit herself a cigarette without taking her eyes off him.

Inge didn't know why she felt so nervous, but she didn't trust this man. However, since moving to the house and suddenly finding herself a young widow she seemed to feel nervous a lot of the time, as though it penetrated every bit of her. Sometimes she had had to place her hand on the wall to calm her frayed nerves. The bricks always helped; to feel the house's solid form beneath her fingers was all she needed.

Henryk watched as the woman placed her hand on the wall, and bile at once burned his throat. He gripped the arms of the large chair and fell back further into it. She must have got rid of his own chair. It had been a damn sight more comfortable than this, expensive though he suspected this chair might be. He had inherited his chair from his mother, and he could still see in his mind the greasy imprint where she would rest her head every night. In fact, as his eyes took in the rest of the room he realised that there was no evidence left at all that he had been ever here. He wondered if all his possessions had been thrown out by this woman, or perhaps some of them sold. He became a little tearful to think of those objects, and the memories that went with them, gone for good.

'Are you feeling better?' she asked him, trying to smile as she did so, but Henryk could see that her attempt to be civil to him was painful.

'Yes, thank you. It would have been easy to have shut the door in my face.' He could see she cringed then, as if he had looked deep inside her and had read those very thoughts. Out of the corner of his eye he had seen a framed photograph, a man in uniform, though the brass frame had a thin layer of dust and strangely enough was turned towards the window. He had to feel sympathy; it was easy to see himself as the only victim. He gripped the chair, attempting to steady his nerves and continued, 'Do you live alone?'

Inge bristled at the question. She was chastising herself for letting this man in. It was a moment's weakness. She had succumbed to that part of her that she battled against and that her husband Franz had tried, in their four-year marriage, to cultivate. She tried to think where she had hidden her husband's pistol, and her eyes darted to a possible hiding place in the bureau, too far she thought for her to edge her way towards without creating suspicion.

'I'm sorry. It's none of my business,' Henryk said, sensing the woman's annoyance and looking at the floor as he spoke.

'My husband is dead, an accident.' Inge inhaled on what was left of her cigarette, and without thinking quickly used its embers to light another one. Saying it aloud, to a stranger, she sensed the irony. All that fighting, and Franz had to go and die under the wheels of an armoured car that was going too fast.

'Oh, I see.' The man had looked up then, and he had stared too long at her for Inge to be comfortable with it. She found it hard to look into those eyes. They seemed too old for the face, as if they had seen so much horror and that if you stared into them for too long, you too would be inflicted. 'Would you mind if I had a cigarette?' he said.

Inge, again acting almost automatically, responded with the politeness of handing him one. She watched as he put it shakily to his lips and lit it. Henryk spluttered a little as he did so. It had been a long time since he had had a cigarette, and the smoke seemed to burn his lungs and the nicotine rush to his brain and make him feel dizzy. But after a couple of minutes his body seemed to reacclimatise itself to the sensation and he relaxed.

'This is my home,' he said. He looked closely at the woman as he said this, but her face remained emotionless. He inhaled, holding the smoke in his lungs for a few seconds before releasing it and continuing, 'Correction, it was. It was taken from me, but it is mine. Nobody has a right to own it but me.' As he spoke, he noticed the cigarette in the woman's fingers was burning dangerously close to her skin. Suddenly she broke from her apparent torpor.

'Get out! This is my home. I've lived here for years,

with my husband before he died. You have no right to come here. What do you think I'm going to do? Leave just because you've turned up? Give you money?'

Henryk, startled by this outburst, tried to find words to say, but none came. How could he explain? He was shaking. It was not her house to live in. It was his. It was his, his alone. When he had not been here, it had called to him, always had. It had staked a claim on his soul the moment he had moved in. Henryk had intended to fill it with children, a good woman, but the house always had other ideas, and in the end he had abandoned these notions of family.

Inge realised she should have never let him in, this Jew who might take her home from her. She belonged here. When Franz and she first moved in she had been unable to sleep one night and had sat restless in that armchair, pushing her head far back into the cool leather, hoping that the change in air would help her relax and maybe doze off. It had spoken to her then, of course not in words, the house was merely bricks and mortar, but she had felt the vibrations. It was rather like falling in love, a revelation that had struck her like a sudden pain. She had walked to the walls and had pressed her cheeks against them. I am yours, it had said, and you are mine. And so the pair had become, more so after Franz died. She tried to regain her composure and speak in calmer tones to the man she now felt a decided hatred towards. 'I think its best that you leave. I'm sorry, really but you don't belong here.' She moved towards him, and in response he rose from the chair.

Before either of them knew what was happening the pair were wrestling together. Her legs wrapped around his. His fingers gripping the still burning cigarette, which eventually dropped to the floor. She had her hands around his throat. It was clear to him that he was not the man he once was, who could have easily fought off this slender woman. He struggled to unhook her hands from around his throat, gave up and instead began flailing with his fists. One blow connected well with her face, caught her in the nose and a thin sliver of blood slowly tricked from one of the nostrils, down to her lip, finally ending its journey on the end of her chin. At this she clawed at his eyes and the man screamed in pain.

Neither saw the fire, insignificant enough to be put out with the heel of a shoe if it had been noticed in time. But the pair were still consumed with their fight, enwrapped like two lovers on the chair, arms flailing, grunts of desperation. Each not willing to give up.

The shiny new Volkswagen eased up the hill and stopped outside the house.

'Marta, I think we're here.' Edmund turned to his wife, who was now too busy swapping her elegant court shoes for a pair of stout walking ones to answer him. She eventually glanced up and pulled a face.

'Are you sure? Here?' She then turned her attention to her head scarf, tightening the knot under her chin with a grim determination.

'It's the right address. Uncle Henryk's house. Mine now.' He corrected himself after a brief pause, 'Ours now.' Marta hadn't even wanted to come with him here today, and it had taken much pleading to get to her to do and a promise of eating out at a restaurant that evening. She now looked appalled at the sight of the house, and he himself felt rather crestfallen. It looked worse than he had expected. The black still clung to it, and the place where the door once was, now was boarded up, along with the spaces where the windows had been.

'Good God!' Marta hissed, shaking her head at her

husband as she spoke. 'So this is it?'

Edmund studied his wife's face, thinking how to make the situation better. He suspected she had hoped for some kind of mansion. Her family were a better class than his, and he found he constantly disappointed her. 'I didn't expect it to look quite so bad, but it ...'

He was interrupted by a sharp prod in his side from his wife. 'Somebody is coming over'

'Please stay away from that building, it's not safe,' the man approaching called out, but he sounded excited rather than stern, and he smiled as he yelled this warning, standing eventually, rather out of breath, in front of the young couple.

He introduced himself as Richard Fleischer, explaining that he lived nearby. As Edmund explained the reason for his and his wife's interest in the burnt house Richard responded saying that he had never heard of a Henryk Ullmann, adding that that might be expected, however, as he had only moved into the area himself a few months ago. Richard, in fact, wasn't particularly interested in listening to what Edmund had to say. He was more interested in telling the story that he had heard.

A young woman and her husband had lived in the house during the war, and she continued to do so when he was tragically killed in an accident. According to neighbours, she became increasingly withdrawn, rarely leaving the house. In fact, on the day of the fire, she had not been seen for several days. It was supposed it was a stray cigarette that had started it, as she was often seen at the window smoking. Richard paused and huddled closer towards the pair. Edmund saw he almost shook with excitement as he relayed the last piece of the story. It seemed the woman was not alone when she died. They found another body, a man the rumours suggested, though again her neighbours had said that they never saw anybody enter the house on that day or any days before it. It was a mystery, and some said that perhaps the husband had not died at all, that she had kept him like some kind of prisoner. He blew out a great puff of air, shook his head, and Edmund caught his wife's horrified expression.

'Well, how horrid. Come on Edmund. Please.' Marta was pulling him away. Edmund had wanted to, at least, take a look inside, but he could see that his young wife was keen to get back to the car, and that if he did insist on staying any longer, he would pay for it later.

'Thank you Richard, quite intriguing really.' Edmund smiled, held out his hand, and it was shaken with some enthusiasm by the other older man.

Richard watched the couple walk quickly away and get into their car. He continued to stand on the pavement, watching the car snake its way down until he could see it no more. Richard remained standing for a few minutes, suddenly gripped with an unexplained fear that they would return, that they would not give up so easily, that they would want to go inside and he couldn't have that. He took out a packet of cigarettes from his pocket and, without taking his eyes off the road, took one and put it to his lips. Only then did he begin to relax. He knew this day would come, it would not be the last time that somebody would try and claim the house, to take it from him. Only he could mend it, make it whole once more. It was his, and he was its. He moved towards it, and touched it, letting his free hand run across the brick, and closed his eyes as the vibrations ran up through his fingers, travelled up his arm. He shivered with pleasure at the sensation. The cigarette continued to burn dangerously near his knuckles, before falling, still smouldering, on the pavement beneath.

The Stranger You Know

Hazel placed her hand on the wall, to steady herself more than anything else. She continued to stare, waiting impatiently for whoever it was to return.

Just moments ago she had seen a distorted shape through the frosted glass pane of her front door. A figure, male she supposed, on account of the height and build. Perhaps they had got impatient; these days she wasn't as quick on her feet. Or maybe they saw her equally blurry form on the other side and realised that the house wasn't empty after all.

But the knocks were confident. There was no sense of urgency, a space of a few seconds between each one, like the steady chimes of a grandfather clock. Hazel wondered what might have happened if she had answered. She caught her breath then, panic, ice cold and jagged shot through her. Her free hand was screwed up tightly into a fist, the skin almost stretched translucent over the knuckles and she stared down at it, as if it didn't belong to her at all.

'Bugger them,' she hissed under her breath.

Hazel eventually let her fist relax, though she still leant on the wall. They thought she was an old fool, that she had lost her marbles like the rest of them around here. Why on earth did they think she'd answer the door at this time?

Hazel thought of that poor woman at number thirty-two. She didn't know the woman to talk to, couldn't even recall her name, but she always recognised a face, and it was certainly her in that photograph in that local free newspaper. Hazel had sat down and read the article eagerly, feeling strangely excited that she knew the person in it. A sorry tale, cuts and bruises, a broken arm. She read the scant details of the attack with a peculiar hunger. Hazel didn't like to admit it, but she felt a kind of pleasure in reading about somebody else's misfortune. She passed the flat only the other day; the curtains were still drawn. Hazel had wanted to knock, but thought better of it. It was best not to get involved in these things.

She stood by her front door a few minutes more before returning to the front room, where she couldn't resist going to the window, straining to see if the ghostly outline of her unexpected visitor would be there. Her fingers fidgeting with the net curtains, hoping she wouldn't be seen.

Hazel hoped that it had been her son.

John came around infrequently, usually when his benefit had run out and he was desperate. She was never quite sure what he did with his money. Hazel suspected that he wouldn't bother visiting her at all if she didn't slip something in his pocket every once in a while.

Anyway, it was just like her John to be impatient. Hazel couldn't understand why he would rush off the way he did. It wasn't as if he had a job, but he always seemed to have somewhere to go. Especially after she had handed him a few pounds.

No, her visitor was more than likely to be one of those kids that hung around the estate constantly, as if they didn't have homes to go to. Most of them seemed to spend their time by that shabby playground. It was a shame really. When she first moved here it had been newly installed, the paint still fresh and gleaming. But one night somebody set fire to the roundabout. Hazel had heard the commotion and had stared out of her bedroom window; it looked like a giant Catherine wheel, the blurred lights and the squeals. The following week the swings were stolen, then somebody sprayed the slide with disgusting words, some Hazel had to ask John what they meant and he had squirmed uncomfortably in the armchair.

Hazel had passed the ruins only yesterday, trying her best not to take any notice of the usual gang of kids, dressed almost identically in tracksuits. One of them, a tall lanky boy, had looked at her, and she in turn had stared defiantly back at him. It was lucky she had her wits about her, though. At first glance he looked like some kind of monster, his face disfigured, large vacant eyes and the jaw stretched down, the mouth wide as if it were screaming. Of course it was a mask, something left over from last month's Halloween. She didn't believe in that nonsense, of course. Carol-singing that was it in her day, not all this stuff from over the water. She told that nice lady on the till at the supermarket the other day that it was nothing more than begging.

But they weren't content with just staring. Hazel was sure it was the one in the mask that started it, yells and a couple of words she didn't like to repeat. She had to bite her lip not to give them a piece of her mind. But she had looked back, just the once. There was somebody else, just standing there, at the back. Dressed in black, not doing anything at all. It was him that had frightened her the most.

A flash of something passed the window. Hazel quickly pulled back not wanting to be seen, but she moved too quickly for her body to cope with, as she had to steady herself on the armchair. She supposed it was that little bugger who'd knocked on her door, and she wondered if she should call the police.

But Hazel remembered the timid young police officer that had paid her a visit after the number thirty-two incident. He was a nice young man, everything about him neat, even his smile. The sort of fellow she would have liked John to have turned out to be, if he had knuckled down. But to Hazel, the young policeman didn't seem to be cut out for the job. Hazel supposed he had watched those cop shows on the television and thought how exciting it all was. Of course, reality was a different kettle of fish. People nowadays had less respect for a man in a uniform, especially around here. Hazel had watched as his hands shook, grasping that mug of tea she had made for him. He took it too gratefully, like he was having a moment's reprieve from that horrible world out there. What could a lad like that really do? Those little thugs, the same ones that hung around that playground, were untouchable. The police could do nothing, she knew that. Not like in the old days when you could give a boy a clip around the ear. Not that it did any good every time, sometimes it made things worse. Some kids were beyond a good slap, even if it was your own flesh and blood.

Hazel was still gripping onto the armchair for support when the figure returned to the window. She watched it fearfully. A few years ago she would have marched up to that window, pulled the net curtains back and rapped on the glass to shoo whoever it was away. Today though, she hung back, wondering if whoever stood there was watching her too.

She supposed it was that kid from the other day, the one that was making the gestures, the one that was the loudest with the cat calls, the sort that took pleasure in shouting out the most offensive of names. Hazel had seen him before. Usually he had others around him; actually come to think of it she had never seen him alone.

An hour had passed, and Hazel was now sitting uncomfortable and stiff on the third step of the staircase. She looked longingly at the armchair, the cushion placed just so. She would have done anything for a bit of relief. She had returned to the front door, anticipating that the kid would return and for some reason she had wanted to be prepared.

Not that Hazel had any intention of answering the door. But it was better than waiting in the chair, of jumping at every little noise. Her fingers twitched and occasionally they would reach out for the phone she had placed by her side. She debated whether to ring John again, as he always had his mobile with him. She had succumbed once and had listened in a tearful desperation to the ringing tone, then, with some relief, heard her son's voice.

'John... it's your mum, John?' But the voice on the other end did not pause; it carried on and Hazel realised that it was just a recording. She ended the call without leaving a message as requested. Where on earth was he? It was so typical of John not to be around when she needed him the most. But that was her son, wasn't it? Just like his father, took what he wanted, didn't care about anybody else as long as he was fine. He was always a difficult child, even as a baby he cried all the time, and his father had been no use to her at all. That's why she didn't miss him when he didn't come home one day. Neither she or John had seen hide or hair of him for years, and frankly she didn't care. She sometimes thought that John treated her the way he did because he blamed her in some way for his father's desertion. Hazel had tried her best. Of course, there had been times when she hadn't been quite the parent she should have been, but nobody was perfect, were they? She was the one who had to pick up the pieces, to get on with life and the responsibility of having a child.

A succession of screams and howls from outside made her jump, and Hazel stared anxiously at the door again. There was nothing there, but she now wondered if she should shut herself in her bedroom and perhaps go to bed early. But she quickly grew indignant towards this idea. This was her home; why should she allow a few kids to dictate where she went and what she did?

She remained sitting there in the pitch black. Though she had got used to the position and was more comfortable, she still felt anxious and occasionally would stare up into the hallway. Perhaps if that kid returned, he'd see the house in darkness and would leave her alone. She shivered. It had got cold in here all of a sudden. Hazel felt the chill a lot lately. This week she'd woken up at the same time each morning and each bit of her seemed frozen, no matter how many blankets she'd piled on the bed. The heating had been on, but she just hadn't been able to get warm.

Hazel wondered if she should call John for the second time. Surely he would be at home by now. But she was struck with a sense of pride and thought better of it. What would he do anyway? It must have been past eight by now and he'd be in that local of his, supping beer, just like his father had done. He'd rung her from there once, the alcohol giving him a guilty conscience perhaps, his words slurred. No, John would be as much use as a chocolate fireguard, and by the time he'd got here it would be past ten. Hazel decided she'd sit it out, even if it meant sleeping where she was.

Somebody passed. She saw their shadow, though they didn't stop this time. Perhaps it was Mr. Sinclair from the flat a few doors down. Nice man, a bit younger than her, but he had a kind face. He would smile and give a little wave when he saw her from afar, and there was something that made her feel sad when he did so. He had a daughter, though she lived in Australia. She remembered him telling her that when they had bumped into one another at the post office a few months back and got talking while waiting in the queue. He missed his daughter, Hazel could tell that. He had pulled out his wallet and proudly showed her a photo of a tall, middle-aged woman who looked tanned and smiling. Hazel hadn't told him about John.

It was quiet now. Unusual, as often it was when it got really late that they started. Often she'd hear a motorbike roaring around and around accompanied by excited high-pitched yells, like those of a bunch of animals. Tonight though, nothing. Strangely it made the hairs on the back of her neck stand on end, and the mild worry that had begun earlier that day had festered and now pulsated through her like an extra heartbeat. She closed her eyes, those tiny bonfires of pain now roared as a great mass, and she rubbed both legs and her hips as vigorously as she could in the hope that it would help.

When she opened her eyes again there was a figure at the door.

Hazel held her breath. A few seconds, that was all she had closed her eyes for and he had appeared out of nowhere. Hazel hadn't even heard his footsteps, but then she'd been preoccupied with her legs, hadn't she? She anticipated his knock, but it seemed he was aware that she was waiting just as patiently behind the other side of the door for him.

She could call the police. The phone so tantalisingly close, but the face of that young officer came to mind. What would they do? They'd probably think she was some batty old woman who was frightened of her own shadow. Hazel recalled the woman she once was. She had a bit of fire in her belly once upon a time, had had to be strong being a single parent, and John wasn't an easy child to raise. But here she was now, shaking like a frightened child in her own home.

'Go away! Go on, I ain't got nothing,' she yelled out, trying her best to make herself sound annoyed, but the sound that came out of her mouth appeared to her so small, and her voice was quivering even before she reached the end of her short outburst. The figure at the door remained motionless. He was doing it to frighten her, that was it. He didn't want any money; he just was playing some stupid game, like all the kids around here. Hazel pulled her lips back tightly into a grimace. Why did he pick on her tonight? Surely he had his fun that other day, humiliating her like that, the big 'I am' in the playground, all his friends around him laughing. He was on his own now; he had no audience, no one to impress.

'Sod off, go on,' Hazel continued, trying again to summon some courage from somewhere, but the figure just appeared to be waiting. Suddenly she wished John were here. Yes, there were times when she regretted the day she had had him, but she needed him now. All six foot of his useless bulk.

Hazel struggled up. Her feet had fallen asleep and felt like two blocks of dead flesh, so she was forced to wait a few minutes before she got the feeling back in them and made a couple of nervous steps forward. She was inches from the door, and studied the shape for a while. She wasn't going to have it this time; why should he terrorise the neighbourhood the way he did? Everybody was afraid, nobody wanted to face him.

So she opened the door.

Hazel could not see the face at first. But as he moved a little further towards her, she couldn't help but smile, if a little sadly.

'Oh, it's you,' she said. 'I thought ..., I thought you were somebody else.' She swayed momentarily, a little hesitation, a quick glance over her shoulder. Then Hazel looked back towards the figure, and saw his outstretched hand. She took it. It felt warmer than she thought it would. He pulled her determinedly towards himself, supposing she might fight it, that she may not want to go.

The pair stepped carefully out into the darkness, slowly, as if they had all the time in the world, and Hazel whispered the house and her absent son a subdued goodbye.

Child of Winter

I

'A month ... that long?' Angela had looked at her husband's smiling face.

'Yeah. Why not? Come on, would be good to get away for a bit.' Simon tried to sound persuasive, but she could sense in his voice that he had already made the decision and they were going anyway. Angela wondered sometimes why he bothered to ask, as most of the time he had no intention of waiting for an answer.

Simon had told her that morning that one of the members from the club had a cottage somewhere in the Scottish wilderness, which he rented out in the summer months, but now was standing empty, as the season was over. He had asked Simon if he knew of anyone who'd like to act as a kind of caretaker for a month, perhaps even more. Angela guessed that her husband had jumped at the chance to volunteer. He was not a man who found retirement easy; he had joined committees, becoming a board member of some charity or another. To Angela, Simon seemed as busy, if not more so, as when he was working. She had wondered if her husband welcomed these distractions. Where once they had been a young couple, working together towards a future, a home of their own and children, retirement had pushed them apart, and now with nothing really in common, they were travelling down very different paths. Their huge three-bedroom house did not help. The pair seem to wander around it, some rooms frozen in time and never used. There was one room in particular, which Angela had realised Simon avoided. She, on the other hand, often found herself nervously hovering around it. Sometimes her hand on the doorknob, wanting to turn it, to step inside, but feeling too frightened to do it. Often she imagined that the room would be the same as it was all those years ago. The cot, still in its packaging, propped up against the wall. That small cupboard with its pastel coloured handles, some of the drawers filled, mostly nappies if she could recall now. Of course Simon had got rid of the cot. He hadn't thought she was watching, but she'd seen him, just a few days after she had returned from the hospital, taking it to the car. The cupboard, she guessed, had followed it quickly afterwards. At the time she had felt angry with him for doing it. There may have been other children; they could have adopted, even fostered? But Simon, it seemed, gave up on the idea that he would ever be a father. Even now the memory of it gave her a shiver down her spine. Of course, grief consumed her less aggressively as she grew older. But it remained always a lingering sadness, a sadness which never really left her.

Perhaps Simon was right. They needed to get away from the house for a while.

Simon blew out a cartoonish puff of air as he lifted Angela's case into the boot of the car. The other sat by her side, which, she didn't like to admit to him, probably weighed a little more.

'Christ, what have you got in here woman?' But he grinned as he said this, and shook his head in mock horror when she indicated the second suitcase, and he added, 'I suppose you hear about people getting snowed in for months up there.'

Strangely her husband's throwaway comment gave her a sharp twinge of anxiety and she looked round at the house, as if she might be seeing it for the last time. No matter what she thought recently, this had been their home for twenty-five years. She was strangely attached to the place, like a lover she had ceased to have any great passion for, but clung to the familiarity of.

For hours, it seemed, they crawled up endless grey stretches of motorway. At some point Simon had turned on the radio, and, with the soothing tones of the presenter, coupled with the gentle groan of the engine, Angela was soon lulled into a deep sleep. When she awoke it was a very different landscape that greeted her.

'Afternoon, you. Nearly there.' Simon smiled, though he didn't let the smile linger long, and quickly resumed his concentration on the road ahead. The change in weather, and these surroundings had made her husband a more cautious driver than he was at home. Angela looked out with bleary eyes. Snow lay on every surface it could, and this white nothingness went on forever. The only indication that, perhaps, she and Simon were not completely on their own was a thin line of smoke that must have come from a chimney of some farmhouse in the distance. It contrasted sharply to the view they had at home, row upon row of houses. When she couldn't sleep she could look out and see a light on somewhere, so it felt as if you were never really ever alone.

'Beautiful, isn't it?' Whilst he said this her husband continued to keep his eyes on the road in front of him, and it could easily have been supposed that he was talking to himself. For some reason he had unexpectedly opened his window a little, and she shuddered as a thin sliver of cold air skimmed her cheek.

It was the sort of picture perfect scene that Angela knew looked pretty on a Christmas card - the reality of it, though, all that space and nowhere to hide. However, she took comfort in Simon's relaxed expression. Those lines around his eyes, which she had observed getting deeper over the past few months, seem to disappear.

The cottage hadn't turned out to be quite how Angela had imagined. In her head she had envisaged an open fire, an old but comfortable sofa in front of it, everything looking a little worn, so she had prepared to make the best of it. In fact, the reality was very different indeed. Inside it was modern, more so than their home back in Harbury. The open fire did not exist. In its place was what looked like a television set, and that Simon switched on as easily as if it were. The sofa was there, but it looked practically brand new, and the variety of suitably coordinated cushions added that touch of style.

'This is nice,' she said.

Simon caught the surprised expression in her voice, and couldn't help but smile a little smugly. 'You see, told you it's going to be lovely.' He put his arms around her, and kissed her on the cheek.

The snow was soon supplemented by a fresh thick covering in the morning. The pair of them had woken up earlier than usual, the dawn intruding without apology through the thin curtains. Simon had jumped out of bed with a bit more vigour than normal, and like a child ran to the window.

'Now, that's snow,' he said.

Angela joined him just in time to see the beginnings of a new flurry, which came down cautiously at first, but gradually began to fall quite steadily. It was not the light, feathery kind they had back home, which melted as soon as it touched the surface of a car or the pavement. This was the kind that settled, building up layers like the tiers of a wedding cake. Flakes so big she could almost see the ridge of their tiny points, and soon there was a fresh, thick covering over everything. A whiteness so bright it made Angela screw her eyes up in discomfort.

'Funny, it doesn't matter how old I am, it still makes me excited,' he continued, and Angela saw the echoes of the son they might have had in her husband's face.

'Perhaps we should build a snowman?' Angela chuckled to herself, turned to look at Simon and was taken aback by his unexpected kiss. His lips lingered, longer than usual, and when he pulled away his hand was still gripping the back of her head, gentle but firm.

'I love you. I know you will never forget about the baby, but neither have I, Angela ... but we have to accept that it's just the pair of us.'

When Angela had returned from the hospital those many years ago, the pain of the loss - the pain that even back then she knew would never go away - was at its freshest and sharpest. Her world had simply ceased to possess any meaning or any joy. Those around her didn't know how to cope with her depression, and sooner or later most of them gave up trying, completely or virtually disappearing from her life - like Simon's sister, Rachel, who in the latter stages of Angela's pregnancy was always calling round and couldn't do enough to help, always ready to offer to help with preparations for the baby's arrival; but after the stillbirth Rachel had more or less stopped calling completely. Perhaps she found the situation too uncomfortable to cope with, talking to the suddenly and cruelly bereaved mother too difficult.

Simon, himself, had been the most doting of husbands. For the first few days he had not let her get up from the sofa, and there had been breakfast in bed every morning.

Then as time went on they went on holidays, had meals out and weekends away. It seemed nothing was too much for him to do.

Yet all Angela had wanted was to become normal again, for the pair of them to acknowledge their dead son. At the time she had believed Simon had accepted the loss and had moved on. But she studied her husband now, and realised that the tears that he attempted to blink furiously away hid the pain he'd been keeping from her all of those years. In the selfishness of her own grief, Angela had forgotten that perhaps Simon had been grieving too, that he had mourned the loss of his son in those awful months afterwards, that even now, the pair of them retired and seemingly used to being a childless couple, he felt the loss of that child, and perhaps the children that never were, as deeply as she did. It had made her want to cry, and she wrapped her arms around him, to comfort herself as much as Simon. After a few minutes he pulled away from her gently.

At Simon's beckoning they were soon outside. He had given Angela hardly any time to pull on her coat, but once outside she suddenly became too lost in the moment to care about her cold ears and fingers that quickly became frozen. Whilst Simon stood with his mouth open and boyishly let the falling flakes dissolve on his tongue, Angela quickly gathered up a ball of snow and with unusual dexterity threw it at her husband. He turned, but was too late for him to respond before it hit him firmly on the shoulder. Angela couldn't help but laugh to see the initial shock on his face, though it quickly turned to a grin. It was only a matter of minutes before the pair of them were throwing icy missiles at each other like a couple of children.

Later, after the daylight had ended sooner than either of them had expected, they huddled on the sofa with mugs of tea and with a blanket they had found in one of the bedrooms. After dinner and soothed by several glasses of red wine they did the same, not talking, but this was more out of contentment than any kind of awkwardness. They held hands as if they were courting all over again, and Angela was almost loath to break the spell when she headed into the kitchen to make the pair of them a coffee.

It was an eerie sight from the kitchen window. There was no light other than the moon, which seemed to be exceptionally bright, so much brighter than it was back home. So at first she thought it was merely this ghostly light playing tricks with her eyes. The kitchen had a chill to it and this added a sharp edge to her nerves, so she jumped a little at the flash of movement that she caught sight of outside. Whatever it was darted in and out of the trees, as if it were playing hide and seek. An animal, it had to be. Some woodland creature attracted by the light of the cottage, perhaps hoping for scraps. Then she saw it clearly, suddenly equally transfixed by the woman staring back at it.

A child, a naked little boy in fact.

'But I saw him, please Simon; he's out there, nothing on in this weather.' She had had to wake Simon up - he had fallen asleep on the sofa - and he stared at her, still a little sleepy and disbelieving his upset wife.

'For God's sake, Angela, really. We are in the middle of nowhere.' He remained seated for a while, rubbing his temples, feeling a little woozy from the wine. After a few minutes he reluctantly got up and stumbled to the kitchen. He returned minutes later, stony faced and very much sober. His lips drawn in to a thin tight line.

'There's nothing out there now. It must have been some wild creature, probably attracted by the light,' he reported, glaring at Angela's concerned face, before trying to smile reassuringly.

'But I saw him, really Simon.'

He had hushed her then, gently easing her into his arms. Angela wasn't sure if the gesture was comforting or patronising, but she realised that Simon wasn't listening to her as she continued trying to explain what she'd seen.

They had gone to bed soon afterwards, but Angela couldn't resist, once Simon had fallen sleep, creeping to the window.

Angela spent the next day listlessly on the sofa. Simon had been cautious around her, and she caught him staring at her with a concerned expression every time she happened to look out of the kitchen window. On one occasion, just as the sun was beginning to set, he had stood behind her, his hands gently resting on her shoulders. Perhaps the gesture was supposed to be comforting, but to Angela it seemed like some kind of warning. And his face with that ever present smile irritated her.

So, she felt a kind of relief when Simon quickly dozed off after dinner. She gave it a few minutes, before quietly taking the dinner plates to the kitchen, supposing she could use that as an excuse if her husband did suddenly awake. She stood then at the window, not letting her eyes stray from it.

It was peculiar experiencing the desperate hopefulness after all these years. In the hospital, before they had induced her, she had felt it, gripping her vehemently, and she had clung to it like a drowning sailor might do to a stray oar; but tonight Angela greeted it with some caution, not quite the old friend she hadn't seen for a long time.

Angela had always carried the feeling she had given up too easily. Though the doctor had told her in plain, emotionless words that she would never be able to carry a child full term, the doubt that perhaps she and Simon should have given it another go always plagued her now and again. A wound that never did heal, so she had an almost dogged determination that she wouldn't give in tonight.

After half an hour Angela couldn't resist any longer, and put on her coat.

The cold quickly found its way in, no matter what. For a brief moment she wondered if she should head back, and put a few more layers on, but chances were it would wake Simon and she was in no mood for what would become an argument.

'Hello ... Is anybody out there?' Her voice fell into the darkness, but she continued to search with quick, eager movements. 'Hello?' It was silent out here. Back at home it was so noisy - police sirens, cars driving past, in the summer the sound of a television escaping from an open window somewhere. Out here Angela could almost hear her heart, and it was rapidly beating at this moment in time. Then, out of the corner of her eye, she caught a flash of something moving. Instinctively she stumbled towards the direction it was heading.

'Please, don't be frightened,' Angela called out desperately. She had cut her hand whilst trying to push her way through the undergrowth, and a thin sliver of blood wormed its way down her index finger. Angela caught another flash of movement, and spun herself around so quickly she became dizzy, and had to hold onto to a tree for a moment or two. She gave a gasp of surprise when something cold took hold of her wrist, and she turned expecting to find Simon standing there.

Instead of her husband, the child stared up at her.

Angela reeled back in horror. The face that stared inquisitively up was that of an old man. The eyes, though large and childlike, were surrounded in a complicated pattern of deep lines, each one the beginning of a new, deeper line. The nose, comically big on that small face, hooked over the mouth. It attempted to smile, though the lips struggled with the effort, and it seemed more like a grimace.

Yet whatever it was, it sensed her disgust and released its grasp. It cowered back, the eyes wide and frightened. The pair of them, inches apart, stared at each other.

At the hospital, a nurse had told her in hushed, soft tones that if she wanted to, she could see her son, say goodbye, so to speak. Simon had not been so keen; he had hovered nervously around the bed, and when she had got up he had rushed to her side as if to push her back down again.

'Don't be afraid,' the nurse had said. 'No matter what, he's still yours.' And she had looked down at this strangely tiny thing wrapped up in a blanket. Angela had not been horrified or repulsed, instead she had gathered up the still baby in her arms, and had traced her finger along his sunken cheek. She had rocked her son, until Simon had suddenly appeared by her side and with a gentle force unpeeled her arms, taking the small bundle away without saying a word.

The lost mother inside of her lifted up her hand and held it towards this strange little creature.

The moment Angela had been told her son was dead she refused to give him a name. Since then she had always regretted it. At the funeral she had realised that Simon had named the child Anthony, and Angela had felt cheated, as it was a name she would have never chosen herself.

'Edward... he would have been called Edward.'

The thing in front of her pulled at her arm.

For a moment she had suddenly remembered Simon, and imagined him still asleep. Perhaps she ought to go back, take the creature. No it was not their son, but still, she could be a mother, she could still give it her love. But it was much stronger than she was, and each time she attempted to head back towards the cottage it pulled her its way a few more steps forward, until it seemed they were deep within the trees, and she couldn't see the cottage itself.

It was then she heard it. Children. Lots of them. Laughter, but among it all was one distinctive cry. That of a baby, new born, she could tell, its mews were high pitched and desperate. And Angela felt herself grip the creature's hand more tightly.

'Mummy's coming, my darling, she is.'

The creature looked up then. And Angela let it lead her on.

II

Simon had not wanted to leave the warmth of the cottage. There was this natural desire to wait, to assume that Angela would return in the next minutes. So he had made two cups of tea, which lay untouched, expecting her at any moment and to receive a look of 'what were you worried about?'

An hour later he was cursing himself for having been so torpid. He had searched the area around the cottage for the third time now, calling her name over and over again, until his hands had become so numb with cold he couldn't feel them anymore. He had become excited when he had discovered some markings in the snow, supposing them to be his wife's footprints, but they led to nothing and he wondered if they had been human after all and not instead belonged to some animal that had been attracted by the light seeping from the cottage. He chastised himself over and over, pacing the kitchen angrily. Whilst he had been snoring away his wife had wandered out there, getting slowly lost in the dark, fraught out of her mind.

Simon had believed she had got better, that those phases of madness that began as months, but in the last ten years had become a week here and there, had gone. The last few days he had seen them trickle back. The wringing of her hands, the desperate stares out of the window, as if she was looking for something lost.

Simon remembered those awful months after they had lost their son. The pair of them trying to adjust after coming back from the hospital empty handed. He had studied his wife with an ever growing anxiety. There had been some tears, but not enough of them, he thought. There had been some anger too; the doctor had warned him about that. But what he hadn't been prepared for was how Angela withdrew within herself, and moved as hollow as a ghost around their home, hardly having any contact with the friends she used to have. He had believed that she was just going through the mourning process, that her grief was very different to his. But whilst he recovered, the sorrow still there but manageable, hers she wore like a pendant, close to her. She was secretive with it. Until it had become too much and had spilled over one day. He had found her in the garden, rocking gently, whispering a lullaby. Angela had never really got better. She was certainly not the woman he had married, though he loved her as intensely as he had done on their wedding day. Sometimes he had caught her lingering outside the locked door of what would have been their son's bedroom. She seemed trapped, caught between her fear and a desperate curiosity. They should have talked about it more over the years. Simon could see that now, though perhaps he had lacked the courage. He had thought about it in those months after, and even before, her breakdown. Perhaps it might have helped, both of them mourning together the baby they had lost. But at the time it seemed there would always be another day for it. Simon had never found the right time and, to be frank with himself, had been downright afraid. He had only seen another woman cry in his life and that had been his mother after his father had died. It had chilled him to the bone; it was torture to be incapable of offering anything that would have made it better. Words were empty, and all those well-worn phrases he could have used seemed futile and insulting.

It had been the same with his wife. His inability to heal her pain made him feel impotent. Of course, he had lost the chance to have a son too, but his loss seemed to fade in comparison to the fact Angela had carried that child for nine months, felt it grow, even move for the first time. That was a connection that no man could fully understand. Lately though, she had seemed a little better. Simon still saw the sadness in those beautiful brown eyes, but sometimes there were moments when he believed that she had come to terms with it, in her own private way. That's why he had jumped at the chance of this cottage. He'd been so busy over the past few years with committees, and even the club, he suddenly wanted to take a step back and concentrate on his wife. Perhaps in the back of his mind he had wanted to talk about Anthony, knowing that it would reopen that wound, but feeling that perhaps, rather than let it fester, it could be healed.

Now it was too late.

Days had passed. Of course, he'd contacted the local police to report his wife missing, and they'd taken plenty of details from him, including things he could hardly see were relevant, like details of their financial affairs when his wife had disappeared leaving all her bank cards behind.

Ominously, they had taken her toothbrush 'just in case' a DNA sample was required for subsequent forensic examination. There had been searches of the local area organised, one of which Simon had joined in, but he doubted he had been any help at all. The loneliness of the cottage was playing havoc with his nerves. He barely slept, and most nights found himself at the window, seeing shapes in the darkness. At one point he had almost believed he had heard a child cry out. Eventually, with the police reassuring him that they were doing all that they could and that searches would continue, he felt it would perhaps be better for his own sanity if he returned home.

Simon had driven home in a languid state, at one point narrowing missing a collision with a car, and he was forced to pull in at the side of the road. Simon sat there, as if dreaming, though the pain was all too real. He thought momentarily that it might have been better if he had been killed. The atheist inside him knew that he wouldn't be meeting Angela in some heaven, but longed for the comfort of blackness, for this pain to stop. It was growing dark when he turned the key in the ignition, and like a man sleepwalking he steadily drove home.

'Simon, I'm so sorry.' Peter had sat squirming, and staring in his embarrassment at his untouched tea. He was a 'stiff upper lip' kind of a man. He and Simon were friends, but it wasn't a friendship designed to cope, or used to coping, with emotional issues, more one built for an occasional drink or an occasional round of golf. Peter was the owner of the cottage, and it was he who had offered it to Angela and Simon for a month free in return for it receiving some caretaking during winter

'It's fine Peter, really I just appreciate you coming over to see me like this, really I do.' Simon wondered if Peter was blaming himself for what had happened.

'I just can't take it all in, Angela ..." Peter's sentence trailed off into nothing. Simon had always wondered if Peter had a bit of soft spot for his wife. They had met briefly over the years, various dances, and the occasional hello when Peter had picked Simon up. Peter was divorced, several years ago and childless like Simon; there was an air of sadness about him.

'Yes, I know.' Simon was not enjoying this at all. He had dreaded telling people, dreaded all the awkwardness that would ensue. He had called up Angela's sister, whose suddenly unannounced wail of grief sent shivers through his spine, and he had yet to venture to the golf club, not quite having the stomach to cope with the pitying looks and whispers. He had called the Scottish constabulary almost every day, speaking to Detective Skene, who had been assigned to his wife's case. His Scottish brogue had a comforting quality in it, yet his words conveyed nothing that gave Simon any hope at all, and the regular phone calls became another chore to dread.

'And what will you do now?' It seemed a peculiar question to ask, but Simon knew Peter was out of his depth here, and it was strangely something he had begun to ask himself.

'I just don't know, really I don't.'

Four weeks had passed, and the weather had warmed up a little. The threat of snow had long evaporated, but instead the world outside Simon's bedroom window seemed to be constantly wet and grey. It suited his mood. There would be something not quite right if every morning he had drawn back his curtains and been faced with blazing sunshine. Sometimes he wondered why he bothered at all. Most of the time he would move listlessly around the house, often coming across something of Angela's, usually one of her earrings, as she had a habit of taking one off and rubbing her ear absentmindedly. He had begun to collect them into a bowl, and it made him smile, if a little sadly, that there wasn't a pair between them. His wife still had not been found, and he battled to retain any hope of seeing her alive again. He played with the fantasy that she still could be out there, lost, surviving somehow; maybe she had fallen and hurt her head, and was staying with some remote farmer not knowing who she was, not remembering the husband she had left behind. His more realistic thoughts fought for control, though, making knots of anxiety in his stomach, ever tighter and more painful.

More and more often he found himself outside their son's bedroom. Simon recalled the time, all those years ago, when with Angela still in hospital, he had gone into the room and wept, then the time a few days later when he had begun to task of removing things that would remind them that there was ever an expectant child, the cot, a chest of drawers, some of the drawers already filled with baby clothes. Simon thought it was for the best, but he always remembered Angela's face when she had found out what he had done. 'Everything is gone,' she had whispered, like she was facing another kind of loss, and he had felt guilty that he had taken upon himself to do such a thing.

That night he had thought he had heard something in the room. Scratching. His heart had begun to race quite suddenly, and he had struggled to breathe. It must have been nothing, of course. Just his imagination. It was strange how your mind worked in the darkness. He wondered if, perhaps, he was heading for some kind of breakdown. Simon had, as he had begun to do often lately, let his hand wander to the empty side of the bed. He wondered if he would get used to sleeping alone. The bed felt strangely empty. Some nights he woke with a start, bolting upright, wondering where Angela was, then suddenly remembering, and then the pain seemed as violent as it had the night she had disappeared.

Rachel had arrived the next day. Simon's older sister had greeted the news in her usual calm manner; upset though she was, she had not become hysterical. As always being the practical older sister, she insisted she would come and stay. Simon had dreaded it at first, but when he saw her Volvo crawl slowly into the drive he felt a peculiar sense of relief wash over him. Rachel was so like their mother, dependable, with a no-nonsense attitude that was much needed in a crisis. And she had gripped Simon tightly before the pair had got into the house.

'Right, you get my bags, and let's put the kettle on.'

It was painful retelling that awful night. Though, of course, he had been over it with the police several times, now with his sister in front of him, he felt vague, wondering after each sentence whether he had missed something.

'Had she been drinking?' If anybody else had said that to him, Simon would have been happy to hit them, but he knew Rachel was trying to piece the facts together, being practical and forcing him into doing the same. He had shaken his head.

'And how was she, I mean no signs of the old trouble?' Where most people had stayed away from, avoided, the subject of Angela's breakdown, Rachel had steamrollered in, gripping the elephant in the room by its trunk.

'No, well not really. She thought she saw something, outside, one night when she was in the kitchen.' Simon had recalled Angela's face. Straining in the darkness, pale, the eyes full of that desperate longing that he knew only the feel of her newly-born son in her arms would satisfy.

'She thought she saw something?' Rachel had placed down her mug of unfinished tea and was studying her brother.

'Yes, out there, in the woods, she said...' He gulped and looked up at Rachel. He had not wanted to tell her, because in a way he wanted to protect his wife.

'She thought she saw a boy.'

Rachel had not said a word after what he told her. She had merely looked at her brother. There had been an uncomfortable moment of silence, and he had suddenly put his head into his hands and wept. It was not the first time he had cried, but this was different. Why hadn't he seen it? He had taken the silence, that icy calmness that surrounded Angela, to be a kind of acceptance of their loss, a sign that the gradual healing process had really begun. But she had never really got better had she? Angela had just said the right things to him, and hid behind the quietness. Their Scottish trip was meant to bring them together again; instead the cold silence, the empty space just made it impossible for her to hide anymore.

Simon awoke the next day with sore eyes and a thumping head, and had laid there till his sister had knocked on his bedroom door at around eleven o'clock.

'I've got to go back, back to the cottage,' he said.

Rachel sat on the edge of his bed, like she had done when they had been children. It was always when he had been naughty and mother had told him off. Strangely he felt like that now, and cowered into the pillows. 'Do you think that's a good idea Simon, really?' She looked at him sternly, but there was a flash of concern in her eyes. Her lips made a nervous twitch, as if they had more to say but were reluctant to do so.

'I have to. Call it closure.' He grimaced inwardly at his own use of that American expression. He wasn't quite sure if it would do that, but he felt he was just going mad here. He was gripped with an impulsive urge to visit the place he had last spent time with Angela. At this moment he wasn't sure if it would be a goodbye. His sister smiled and nodded her head.

'OK, but I'm coming with you. You're not going there on your own.' She suddenly stretched forward and grasped his hand. It was an unusual gesture for an otherwise practical but unemotional woman, and one which touched him more than he conveyed.

They took Rachel's car, Rachel doing the driving. It was unusual for Simon to find himself a passenger. Angela never drove again after she came back from the hospital. She had never been the most confident of drivers beforehand, but she had enjoyed the little excursions she made into town or visiting friends further afield. After her breakdown she had insisted that they sell her little red Beetle, shaking her head quite violently when he attempted to convince his wife - secretly hoping that she would relent with the decision to part with the car - that perhaps she should take a final spin in it before he advertised in the local paper. In retrospect the sale of her car was a clear sign of his wife retreating from the world. He chewed his lip in frustration now, to think there again he had not seen those warning signs.

The long journey back to the cottage was uneventful. As they got nearer to their destination Simon rarely took his gaze away from the landscape. The snow was there, but looked dingy, and there were snatches of brown vegetation here and there. It had seemed so magical when he had travelled up here with Angela. Now the great expanse of Scottish countryside made his skin crawl, and he had a sudden desire for the bricks and busy roads of his little town.

Unused to being a passenger, Simon felt quite nauseous by the time they actually got to the cottage. He had watched with a growing nervousness the familiar road that led up to the cottage, sometimes craning his neck as if he might catch sight of something. All this time, a bit of him, that logical part of his mind, told him briskly and without emotion that Angela could not be alive. It had been bitterly cold that night; he recalled how his hands hurt with it after an hour or more, how the cold air found its way into small holes in his clothing, slivering its way into coat arms, even under the collar of his shirt. He had been shivering and only the need to find his wife kept him going.

'You OK, Simon?'

Rachel had touched his arm gently and he had become tense, his body rigid, pushing himself against the car door, hiding like a child from an imagined bogey man.

'Simon!' his sister exclaimed, and her sharp tone brought him back round to a more grounded reality.

Simon turned the key in the cottage door with a shaking hand, and he hoped that Rachel hadn't noticed how violently the hand shook. It was strange to stand in the hallway. He suddenly realised it reminded him of the time he had come back from the hospital, knowing that there was to be no baby to welcome into their home. Rachel had been with him then, and just as on that night she walked briskly into the kitchen ready to put the kettle on.

'Do you think she's still out there, Rach?' He looked searchingly at his sister, knowing the answer but wanting to hear a comfortable lie to sooth him. But Rachel would not look back at him; only when the kettle began to boil did she raise her gaze, and Simon saw what she believed in her eyes. It mirrored the awful truth that had been taking an ever firmer grip of him during their journey.

The pair of them ate in a stilted silence - they had brought groceries with them for a few meals. Only occasionally would either one of them make some kind of mundane comment, on the weather or how Simon would always leave his potatoes till last. Simon had no real appetite. He pushed his food around his plate, his sister watching him, holding back on saying anything significant at all. Eventually Rachel swept up his unfinished plate, and with hers took them to the kitchen.

Later Simon found himself staring out of one of the windows into the night. 'It's so dark out there, so odd, no street lights, no cars,' he muttered to himself. 'Poor Angela out there alone.' As if trying to pull himself out of his own stupor, he announced loudly, 'I'm heading out for some air.' He grabbed his coat, walking briskly to the front door and ignoring the worried call of his sister from behind.

It was cold. It began to bite as soon as he shut the door, so he pushed his hands deeper into the pockets of his coat. He wasn't sure what he had expected to find out here, but Simon had this overwhelming urge to get out of the house. He couldn't bear any more silence or polite conversation, though he knew Rachel was only doing her best. She was a good person, the sort you could rely on; he recalled Angela saying that to him once, though the two women were poles apart.

'Angela! ANGELA!' He didn't know why he called out suddenly like that. Simon knew there was no chance that she would answer or suddenly appear from out of the undergrowth, but he wanted to say her name out loud. She had seemed to melt into his mind since her disappearance, and he had this ridiculous idea that perhaps she might fade away completely, like she was never here at all. He remembered his own mother. He couldn't even remember what she sounded like, and now really, most of the images he had of her in his mind were ones that he was sure came from old photographs. Simon didn't want Angela to be like that; he just wanted to hear her voice again.

He caught the flash of movement from the corner of his eye, and thought that he was just seeing things. Only when it appeared again, tantalisingly close enough for Simon to see its complete form, did he realise it was not his imagination. A child. Naked, darting in front him, and then disappearing into the undergrowth again.

'Hello.' Was this what Angela had seen? It did look like a boy, and Simon felt suddenly guilty. He hadn't believed his wife. He thought she was having one of her moments again, one of those moments she had after their son had died. Once she had woken him up, shook him quite violently and told him that the baby was crying, that it wouldn't stop she could hear it. There was another rustle somewhere behind, and he turned around abruptly. But he moved too quickly for himself; before he knew it he was on the floor, his ankle awkwardly twisted and now throbbing with pain. He attempted to get up, but before he knew it there was something balancing on his chest. The boy. Though it wasn't quite that, was it? The same size as a child, and hairless. He caught its face as it leant down to study his own. This close up, he could see its skin was lined and rough like that of an old man and not like that of any kind of infant. And then it opened its mouth in a callous, imbecilic grin and revealed sharp pointed little teeth. This was no child and Simon attempted to recoil back in horror, but the thing pressed heavily down. He thought of Angela.

'What have you done with my wife?' Simon attempted to push the creature off, but it bit him hard on the hand, hard enough for the skin to break, and he winced in pain. A second attempt was more successful, but as Simon struggled to his feet he realised that he and the creature were no longer alone. There were two behind him, several more in front. Boys, or so it seemed at first glance, or to a woman who had lost a child. Small hairless bodies that bore the old, wizardly faces of elderly men. He heard it too then. A baby's cries. But it was a child. It was a call to the others, he supposed.

They watched him. And he crouched, transfixed like a deer caught in the highlights of a car. That sound again, that cry. Poor Angela, had she heard it? What must she have thought? He looked back. The cottage, he could see the light from the kitchen. Rachel.

Rachel heard the yell. She'd been drying the last of the plates, stacking them back into the cupboards as she always did when she stayed here, then folded the tea towel over the taps of the sink, knowing full well that it would still be damp in the morning. She looked out into the darkness, wondering if that had been Simon, supposing that he had discovered them, or more than likely they had seen him first.

Probably so. They had been there since the light faded. Waiting, as they always did.

She had discovered this place and them all those years ago. A walking holiday. The cottage hadn't been in such good repair when she had discovered it, had it? Abandoned, but still a good solid building, just needed a bit of time and money spent on it. They were an unexpected extra, and she didn't mind, did she? Not at first. The child of winter. Winter's children. That's what Rachel had called them. They didn't seem to appear in the summer. She supposed they didn't like the light evenings, or the sun. She always wondered how those hairless, naked little bodies didn't feel the cold, but they revelled in the icy Scottish air. Perhaps they didn't feel anything at all.

The baby had supposed to be a present. A first born, a boy. Then Simon's son had died, not even got to his first year and she had promised them a gift. They had been angry. Rachel would have given her own if she could have had them. But she had done her best. Children go missing. A mother can look away for a split second, and that's all it takes doesn't it? So many of every week. Every year.

But guilt was a funny thing. It spread like a cancer through Angela. So she had sold the cottage. Tried to put it behind her, to forget those children, but she often thought about them. About what she had done. Coincidence. A hand, Rachel hadn't quite expected to be played. The new owner of the cottage knowing Simon like that. A more God-fearing women would suppose that there were higher forces at work. Karma, like a circle and now here she was.

It had been a long time, hadn't it? Perhaps, they had mistaken Angela for somebody else. Somebody who had loved them, given them gifts. Rachel shivered, trying to push that thought away.

Every Queen Deserves a King

The floor was cold and hard against Hilary's cheek. She tried to move in an attempt, impossible though it seemed, to make herself comfortable. But no matter how hard she struggled, to will her head to turn, a force real or imagined was holding her down.

Hilary had supposed that she had only closed her eyes for a minute. There had been a desire to sleep, an overwhelming urge to lose herself in that darkness. But something appeared to be pulling her back, the same something that held her down, that wouldn't let her move. So, she was forced to stare up at the tubes of fluorescent light, though it hurt her eyes. She heard someone speaking her name.

'Nurse Robson?' The sister smiled, without much warmth at Hilary. 'How has your day been so far?' Her tone suggested that she wanted a short and positive response to this question, rather than any kind of truth from the nurse standing in front of her.

'Good, sister. It's been busy so far.'

Sister Harrison nodded her head, and walked away as briskly as she had arrived. Hilary realised that the sister must ask this question, out of duty rather than from any kind of genuine interest, to every new nurse that had begun at St Helens.

Hilary had studied the girl in the mirror that morning and had not quite recognised the reflection. Long brown hair, usually worn down in messy waves, was now pulled back tightly into a ponytail. Her face devoid of any make-up looked much younger than her twenty-eight years and strangely vulnerable. At the interview she had fidgeted awkwardly as she faced questions, which were anticipated but still daunting in reality when they were asked. Why had she left her last job, the year break from nursing? To keep her emotions from bubbling up to the surface Hilary tried her best to answer in calm measured tones.

'And how would you feel, being in the same environment, facing that kind of situation again?'

She had studied the man who had asked this question. His brows raised, the eyes inquisitively studying her to see if she would give anything away. Hilary knew that the response her heart would give may cost her the job, so she gave them something she had prepared. The answer that she had practised so hard in the mirror that she almost began to believe in it herself. 'I'm in a better place now, and have learnt a lot from the experience,' she replied, smiling as broadly as her doubting mouth would allow her to.

'Nurse... nurse ...' The woman had gripped her wrist tightly when Hilary approached the bed. For somebody so otherwise frail she had quite the grip on her, and Hilary winced as she unhooked the bony hand as gently but firmly as she could.

'Ethel, how can I help?' On her first day Hilary had been told by Sister Harrison that she would prefer it if nurses didn't address patients by their first names, but the old woman stared up at Hilary with such frightened, birdlike eyes that she could not bring herself to be so formal. In this particular instance there was no sense in being politely respectful, especially to a woman who, Hilary could clearly see, was running out of time. Of course, there would be the few who didn't appreciate this. Mr. Hargreaves, who had given her such withering looks on her first day that Hilary scuttled around him like a frightened schoolgirl. Then there was sour-faced Ms. Simpson in the bed in the corner, who refused to acknowledge her at all, but then she treated all the nurses like that and would only speak to the doctor who made the ward rounds.

Then there was Mr. Charles Spencer.

He had been admitted on the day that Hilary had begun her first shift. He never once stirred from the foetal position that he had been contorted into when he had arrived. There was an air of mystery regarding this particular patient, and the only information Hilary had obtained about him was from the other nurses.

Charles Spencer had been found alone. He was unwashed, and it seemed the clothes he wore were the only possessions he had. There had been no evidence of any family, and the neighbour who had come out when the ambulance had arrived claimed that no one left or entered the house. Strangely enough, she had not been the person who had alerted the authorities.

It was not these depressing facts, though, that made Hilary more attentive, or that she was as equally alone in the world that made her more sympathetic than the other nurses. There was something about Mr. Spencer that reminded her of another patient, one she had made such a grave mistake with. Though fearful, she was in equal measure determined not to make the same mistake again. But it was a relationship that was one-sided. Mr. Spencer remained like a sleeping baby, and Hilary supposed it was only a matter of time before she would come in one day to find an empty bed.

Ethel, who had quickly become the ward's eyes, had grabbed Hilary by the arm one morning a few days after Mr Spencer had been admitted, and had pulled the nurse closer towards her.

'He was shuffling last night, and moaning. All that noise kept me awake.' She smiled though, her eyes sparkling and excitable. 'I got up to tell him to shush and he hissed at me like... a snake.' She shook her head, revelling in the drama that she supposed her observations might provoke.

Mr. Spencer was still curled up, but Hilary realised that he had indeed moved. He'd been facing the corridor when she had finished her shift yesterday, and now was curled the opposite way, so that the drip was twisted awkwardly over his arm. His expression too had changed. He had once appeared almost tranquil, apparently happy to be in his dark world. Today that same face wore a look of pain, like he was being tormented by some bad dream.

'Mr. Spencer?' There was slight movement. Hilary, on closer inspection, thought that she saw his lips move a little, so she moved closer. 'Mr. Spencer, can I make you more comfortable?' She reacted with a start when he actually spoke.

'Say it's nearly time, Evie.' The voice was strained, and the effort visibly hurt him.

Hilary waited, hoping to hear something more, but his lips remained shut. Instead she heard Ethel's voice from behind her.

'I bet he's never really been asleep all this time,' Ethel tutted.

The woman had appeared the next evening. Hilary may have never known of her existence, if it wasn't for the fact that one of the agency nurses had failed to turn up.

'I wouldn't normally ask, but well I'm sure you would be keen to help out, especially as it's your first week,' Sister Harrison had said, giving Hilary a questioning look, and Hilary quickly realised that if she said no, it would probably be held against her in the months ahead.

'Of course Sister, I'll be happy to lend a hand.'

Hilary had found the woman standing by Mr. Spencer's bed just after ten, and it had made her jump a little.

'I'm sorry, but our visiting hours are over.' The woman did not respond, so Hilary took a cautious step forward. 'I'm really sorry...' She had only just touched the woman's shoulder very lightly, but it was enough for her to turn around sharply and grip Hilary's wrist so tight she gasped in pain.

'I'm aware,' the woman spat back like an angry cat, and if she hadn't held Hilary so firmly, the nurse would have backed away in fear.

Imprisoned to the spot Hilary was able to study her captor. The face that glared back at her was beautiful, but there was something almost too perfect about those features, like she was staring at a mannequin rather than flesh and blood. Hilary guessed that the woman was around thirty, but there was an older air about the way she held herself. And something else, a feeling that grew steadily, and something Hilary had not experienced for a while - an attraction, nothing sexual but a need for this woman to like her in some way, like a younger sibling wanting to impress her older, more sophisticated sister. But tinged with this unexpected admiration was an anxiety, a slow growing fear that crept around her body like the blood in her veins.

'I'm sorry.' The woman let go of her wrist, but it had left its mark and Hilary rubbed the smarting skin. 'It's just the rules I'm afraid, but as you are here.' The woman smiled then and the unnatural mask was no more.

'Thank you. It's just time; its running out, you see.' She then turned and stared for some moments at the curled up man. Mr. Spencer did not acknowledge his visitor, even when she perched herself on the end of the bed. Hilary had left the pair alone, feeling awkward to stand guard over what was obviously a private moment.

In the morning, as she was about to finish her shift, Ethel beckoned her over, giggling like a child with a secret.

'That woman was whispering to him for ages and he was answering her... whisper, whisper, whisper all night... kept me awake.'

It was several days later that Hilary encountered Mr. Spencer's female visitor again. It had been a difficult week. Poor Ethel had died, some kind of seizure. They had found her out of bed and a heap of twisted limps on the floor. She had apparently not died peacefully; there was a look on her face that it was rumoured had so frightened and upset one of the nurses that she had to be sent home. Hilary could not help feeling upset too, as, having no grandparents of her own, she had grown fond of Ethel.

'Good evening,' Hilary said to the visitor, wondering how long the woman had stood beside her. 'There is not any improvement to Charles, I mean Mr. Spencer, I'm afraid.' The woman looked down, and Hilary felt a wave of guilt. This was one of the hardest parts of working in this particular kind of ward. Though inevitable, it was always painful to tell a hopeful daughter or son that all the hospital could do now was to keep their parent comfortable, rather than find any kind of cure.

'I can see that. So have you worked here long?' It was as if the woman had sensed Hilary's uneasiness, and, like she was playing a part, had begun to smile with a little more warmth, and the arms, once crossed over her chest defensively, now hung relaxed by her side.

'A few weeks, I've just moved to the area.' Hilary had found it strangely comforting being in a place where nobody really knew your name. It wasn't like it was back in Oldbury, where she had spent most of the twenty-eight years of her life. Even after university she had moved back there, and had begun her nursing career in the very hospital she had been born in and where her mother had spent the last month of her life. It was the place where she grew from being a nervous student to a nurse, who it had been hinted by the sister at the time, was set to go high in her profession. But, of course, that was before that fateful day when everything had changed. Now she could walk down a corridor, or enter the ward, and there wouldn't be glimmer of recognition. Hilary did not miss those familiar smiles, because they came with eyes that pitied her, or even worse were heavy with accusation.

'We've been here for some time.' There appeared to be a trace of regret in that voice, which led Hilary to believe it wasn't entirely her choice in the matter. 'My name is Evelyn, by the way. We haven't been introduced, have we?' She then held out her hand, and Hilary shook it shyly.

'I'm sorry I can't give you any more details about Charles. You'll need to speak to the doctor on duty; he'll be doing his round in the morning.' Hilary caught the flinch of the woman's shoulders.

'I can't be here then. I have other commitments.' Evelyn pursed her lips tightly.

'I could get the doctor to call you, if you like?'

Evelyn was sitting on the bed now. She was taking Charles Spencer's hand and was slowly stroking it, delicately tracing the knuckles and then gently forcing the fingers to intertwine with her own.

'Your father is in the best place, I assure you,' Hilary

continued, but at this the woman turned slowly around and gave the nurse a look of indignation.

'Nurse, Charles is my husband.' Then she opened her mouth wide and revealed a pair of sharp pointed teeth. The woman's gaze held her, and Hilary felt transfixed, like a fly caught in the sticky entrails of a spider's web. 'I suppose you want to know all about us, don't you nurse?'

'But...' Hilary gulped hard; her mouth was dry and it almost hurt her to swallow. A ball of fear was slowly tightening in the pit of her stomach, and she had a desperate urge to pee.

'Well, perhaps you ought to take a seat my dear; go on sit down on that chair.' There had been no hand to guide Hilary; no one, it seemed, pulled her in the direction of it. And yet she walked reluctantly towards it, putting one foot in front of the other, like a child learning to walk. 'Charles has always been a man who knows his own mind, very stubborn.' Evelyn's face was taunt and angry, yet she never let it spill out; instead it simmered under the surface of her skin. 'And when you have lived on this earth as long as the pair of us have, nurse, you have to have your games, because there is so much time, so many nights, so many years to fill.'

Hilary suddenly realised that Charles was no longer still. With eyes wide open his hand was gripping his wife's tightly, and a moan suddenly could be heard.

'Charles,' his wife responded, but it seemed a command more than anything else. Hilary watched as he slowly, but determinedly, lifted himself up and leant on his wife. His features were sharp and angular, all straight lines in contrast to the soft and rounded features of Evelyn. Curled up for days, he had appeared to be a man who had given up. This new energy forced Hilary further back into her chair.

'Mr. Spencer, please, be careful.' But the man ignored her warning and attempted to stand up, and precariously again gripped his wife for support.

'Well, Charles, you heard what the nurse said.' He smiled then, those cracked lips gradually opening a little wider and a thin, rasping snigger escaped. 'And I have to say, your victory is well deserved my darling. You did very well.' Evelyn laughed, putting her hand up to her mouth girlishly. 'This one thought you were my father.' She gave Hilary a brief nonchalant bob of her head, and like a playground bully smirked to herself. 'Really though, I'm the older one.' It was then Charles's turn to laugh, but it was a breathless attempt, and took so much effort his head flopped listlessly down to his chest. Evelyn quickly cupped his chin, and she supported it briefly before she withdrew and it wobbled a little before gaining its balance once more. 'Yes Charles, the game is over; you've won. It's time for your reward.'

He was trying to say something. Hilary watched his throat contort and the lips move.

Evelyn began to help her husband out of bed. It was some effort, but she was stronger than her slender frame suggested. The pair did a clumsy dance before Charles was actually standing, aided still by his wife. Yet he was suddenly becoming a little less frail than he was a few moments ago.

'Nurse, I need you nearer,' Evelyn said. Hilary had wanted to remain in her seat, and even though she used every bit of energy in her body to keep herself grounded on the chair, she was propelled up against her will and trembled in front of the pair. 'Don't just stand there, you silly girl, help me for Christ's sake.' Against her will, Hilary did what she was told. With strange mechanical movements her arms lifted up and hooked underneath the old man's armpits. She quickly looked behind, hoping that somebody was watching this peculiar scene and would at least alert another nurse. But everybody appeared to be asleep, and reluctantly she returned her attention to the task in hand. 'Right, we need to move Charles to that chair. Come on, girl.' Evelyn did not raise her voice, but its tones were sharp, heavy with authority, and Hilary again found herself doing as she was commanded, eventually manoeuvring Mr. Spencer until he sat awkwardly in the very chair in which she had been moments earlier.

His eyes were bright and enthralled with the nurse standing in front of him. But there was something else there too, altogether more sinister, like a hunter observing his prey. Hilary had the feeling that if she looked too long within their dark depths, she would be lost within them and never see the light of day again. Hilary had spent so many hours looking into the eyes of those on the brink of death and sometimes fearing it. Charles Spencer did not look as if he feared dying at all; he was fighting it tooth and nail, and at this precise moment in time winning the battle.

It was then she felt herself move forward. Her legs, no matter how she fought against it, continued to push her nearer the man, whose arms now were raised and appeared to be welcoming her into them. His hand was suddenly gripping the back of her head, pulling her even closer. Hilary felt his dry lips on her own and then a tongue, foreign and unwelcoming, force its way into her mouth and explore each crevice.

'Now, now Charles what have I told you about teasing?' Evelyn laughed, but there was a tense edge to it and her husband must have sensed it, as he pushed Hilary's face abruptly away. The stale taste of him remained, though, and he did not stop exploring. That tongue travelled down her neck, leaving a thick, glutinous trail of spittle. The mouth opened; she felt his lips, the rough edges of broken skin brush against her neck, causing a hackle of goose pimples to erupt. And then he bit. Hilary felt the skin break, but it was seconds after that the real pain began. A sharp searing heat that gradually gripped her so that she blacked out completely.

The floor was cold and Hilary struggled to focus at first, and wondered whether perhaps she was dreaming. But she didn't remain there for long; somebody was lifting her up, a gently soothing motion like a mother with her child. So Hilary almost gasped in surprise to find Evelyn's face glaring down at her.

'Come on now,' she purred. There was softness in her voice, which contrasted sharply to the eyes that were cold and unblinking. Hilary soon realised that, in fact, Evelyn was not talking to her but Charles, who was stumbling forward. He was not the same man that had been admitted to the ward. Although still wrinkled and swaying clumsily, there was a new energy with which he now approached the nurse on the floor. 'Finish up. Come on, don't let it go to waste.' He fell to his knees at this instruction, so hard that Hilary heard the loud crack as he landed on the floor with a heavy bump. 'Your abstinence is over. Really, my darling, I didn't think you would last this long.' Charles again loomed closer, lips, still as thin as wire and now caked with dried blood, smiled. He gave Hilary a final look, and with his free hand wiped away the single tear that was escaping down her quivering cheek.

You Were Always on My Mind

I raise my hand, wave frantically until Paul returns the gesture. It's comical, like we're meeting for the first time, as if we haven't spent a long and muggy hour in the car together. Most of the journey made in silence, words dangling on the tip of our tongues, but each of us too frightened to make that first move. Perhaps we should have put the radio on, but then it would have only emphasised the awkwardness between the two of us. Accentuated the anticipation that something awful is about to happen.

I continue with my self-conscious wave, though Paul now has turned away and is staring hesitantly at the car. He is wondering whether he had locked it, and eventually succumbs to this niggling suspicion and returns to tug at the door several times. This always makes me smile, even today despite of it all. It's his ritual you see, one of his strange little habits that I have observed over our relationship. Then he walks towards me with determination, as if I'm somebody he must reach, like his life depends on it.

I'm filled with hope.

The sunlight has caught those flecks of ginger in his otherwise blond hair. It has bought out his freckles in the most peculiar of places. There is an almost perfect line of them over each eyebrow, a scattering on his earlobes. Strangely, there isn't a single one on his nose. In this light he glows. It is such a contrast with me, though the two of us have always seemed like polar opposites. I'm dark, my hair chestnut brown, which in the dullest of the winter months can appear almost black. My skin too is olive and, unlike Paul's, the sun makes mine darker if I allow myself to sit in it for too long. There is some Italian in my family, on my father's side I was once told, though my mother has the same chocolate coloured eyes as mine. Paul told me that's what attracted him, my almost exotic colouring in a sea of blondes.

Today Paul is wearing a slim fitted T-shirt, one I'd bought him last birthday and I thought made him look a little thinner than he is, his favourite jeans and those awful plastic shoes that he insists are more comfortable in the summer and that I detest with a passion. Today I'm determined not to mention them, but my irritation simmers under the surface, and occasionally manifests itself with a withering look.

His palm is wet with perspiration when he holds my hand. There is a nervousness about the gesture. I grip him tightly also, forcing my fingers around each of his digits, as if I'm afraid to let him go, that if I do loosen my grasp that he will disappear, and the space that began to swell during our car journey will engulf me completely.

The truth of the matter is that Paul and I haven't been getting on recently. What began as petty bickering, tiny pinpricks of criticism subtly fired, permanently hangs over us both. Those small disgruntled wisps now a great black cloud that threatens overhead.

There have been two big arguments. One so awful, that Paul walked out, slamming the door so hard that it seemed to shake within its frame. He didn't return till later, swaying clumsily towards our bed, me curled up tightly in the corner of it and seething with rage.

Today is meant to be a kind of truce, because I'm sure that we love each other still, and there is a small part of me that believes that this is just a glitch, and because it was Paul that suggested it. He thought it would be good to get out of the flat, that the fresh air perhaps would blow all that ill feeling away.

But there is something still looming, crackles of electricity like the beginnings of a storm, the undercurrents of thunder in the air.

The walk we are doing now is familiar to both of us. Ironically, it's where we had our first date, the weather so very similar to today. Oddly I'd been thinking about it, reminiscing, trying to piece it together in my mind - the way Paul looked, what he'd been wearing. Lately, you see, those early days appear to be lost, like they belong to something I've read in a book or seen in a film and not connected to the couple that we have become. Today I thought we may try to rediscover it, a treasure hunt for love lost.

Paul has loosened his grip and is walking ahead of me now. The light has surrounded him, nothing but a halo of bright yellow sunshine. I have to squint to find him, to see his familiar shape, and it's this I find myself walking with urgency towards. When Paul turns he smiles, and I think to myself, this is how I should remember him, always like this.

We must be nearer the road than I first thought. There's an ear piercing squeal as a car unexpectedly brakes, but gradually it fades away and we are alone once more.

The path is familiar - though I still instinctively follow Paul - and appears to be a little more overgrown than when we were here last. It was late August, our second date and the sky had been holding on fast to the remains of a summer that was slowly fading away. Though still warm, there was that edge in the air that things were changing. Well they were for me, I knew then that I had fallen in love, that what had begun as a mild flirtation across a bar, and had continued when we had gone out for that drink together, had become so much more. Strange how I have forgotten that, my feelings in the beginning. I was once so sure. It has been misplaced as we have become lost in conflict, in yelling, in the frustration of trying to prove to the other that we are the one in the right.

Today, at this moment, all that is forgotten. It is spring not a dying summer. There is instead a promise in the air of brighter days. There are green shoots everywhere, glistening with the rain we have had over the past few days. I'm a believer of signs, of omens good and bad. This is one of them. Paul and I will be ok, I'm sure.

Wet foliage brushes past my naked legs, which make me shiver a little, but it's my own fault. I'm wearing a short skirt, really more suitable to the warmer weather, but today it seemed so promising out there. Paul gave me a look, disapproval hesitantly waiting on his lips. He doesn't like the skirt, thinks it looks cheap and shows that little too much. There, you see, the discord like a badly played note. I put the skirt on knowing it, finding a twisted satisfaction in the knowledge that he would disapprove.

There has been a lot of that of late. Little criticisms, comments made about a burnt dinner, my perfume too strong, the way I make coffee. Sometimes I feel I can do nothing right. In the last few weeks, I have ceased to even try. There doesn't seem to be any point.

It's hard, because once upon a time Paul made me feel the centre of his world. No man has ever made me feel like that. That's why I let my barriers down a bit, let him in gradually. Of course, he now fills every inch of me, that's why I've found all this so hard to deal with. I have this feeling that if it's over and Paul's no longer part of my life, what am I really left with? - an empty shell, that's what.

Perhaps I should have listened in the first place to that voice in my head, the one that rationalises even the most chaotic of situations. I fell in love, though. I didn't listen.

Paul is smiling to himself, just like he was the first time I saw him. It's as if he knows the punch line to a joke, but is keeping it to himself. I used to like it, but lately I suspect there is something more sinister in the expression, that in fact he has some secret that he is hiding from me, and he has been doing so for a long time.

The pain across my chest is so intense it takes my breath away, and I'm forced to stand still. It continues to pull tightly, and only when I close my eyes and talk calmly to myself does it lessen.

So I walk on, trying my best to catch up with Paul, who strides ahead of me.

We do need to talk. There had been another argument; I can't even remember what it was about. I think Paul might have suggested that we end it, but it was one of those throw away comments, meant to hurt, to inflict a moment of pain. Although this was several days ago, that remark still hangs between us. We are on the brink of another fight, the pair of us pacing around each other like a couple of hungry tigers.

My parents had a difficult relationship. There was always tension in the air, as taut as an elastic band about to snap. As a child I used to think it was my fault. It's silly, but I wonder sometimes whether that whatever made my parents unhappy is now following me. An illness that is determined to soil anything good in my life; it clings like a frightened child, and won't let go no matter how hard I try.

The sun is so strong; it hurts my eyes. I can't see Paul, though I'm aware he's in the distance somewhere. In fact, everything seems to be on fire, and I'm sweating fiercely. I want to close my eyes, but when I do the darkness seems to last longer than I want it to.

When I open them again Paul is gone. I'm alone. I call out his name, but instead the panic comes, fierce waves of it crashing over me; I'm drowning. My inner voice tells me to relax, but the anxiety is too strong and that voice becomes lost. I want to see Paul again, to say sorry; I need to say those words and things I know will be alright again.

Another car, in the distance, but it seems to be getting closer. It's speeding, the brakes screech and I turn swiftly around. I can't move now. Something restrains me from pushing forward, and after a few minutes I no longer fight it. I close my eyes, but again the darkness does not help, because I can hear Paul screaming, a sound so awful I feel I'm crying out myself.

When I let the light in the pair of us are in the car. Paul is saying something, mean horrible words spitting out like needles. I grab the wheel, just to make him look around; I need him to see that he is hurting me.

I just want him to stop.

Then suddenly the world is upside down, my head hurting, my legs twisted underneath me. Paul is finally looking at me, but his eyes are glassy, two pools of undisturbed water. He is dead. I have killed him. Again panic rising up, so I begin to count his freckles, the ones above each eyebrow, five... four... three... two... one.

'Becky?' My eyes snap open. 'We're back now, Becky?' I feel Dr Mistry's hand on mine. It's soft and reassuring, though it seems I have only been sleeping. 'You've done very well today, really well.' Dr Mistry leans back on her chair. 'You talked about Paul today, about the accident.'

Paul. I should know this name, something tells me I should know who he is. I study Dr Mistry. She is smiling, like she knows something, the punch line to a joke that she is not going to tell me.

Calaveritas
(Little Skulls)

Billy watched his dad cautiously. His dad was in one of his moods, his brow more furrowed than usual, the face contorted into a scowl that it seemed had been etched there since the day before yesterday.

He watched as his dad lit a cigarette and inhaled it so deeply that he gave the impression that this might be his last one ever, but obviously it wouldn't be. He watched him check his packet of cigarettes. It was relatively full, and Billy had a bet with himself that his dad would smoke another one before leaving the house. There was no can of lager tonight - that was a good sign. Billy hoped and prayed he would be out the house soon.

Billy could never quite understand his dad's work patterns, and assumed he must have a very understanding boss. Several weeks would go by and his dad would sit rarely moving from his favourite armchair, the cushions of which were well worn and frayed at the edges, rather like its almost constant occupant. Then, there would be a glut of weeks where Billy's dad would be up and out of the house.

Billy looked forward to the times when his dad was not there. Although even when his dad was gone, the man's presence seemed to linger somehow for a while, leaving not just his cigarette smoke hanging in the air. Often Billy would have to creep around his dad, trying not to make any noise; though he quickly discovered that often just his presence was enough to make his dad snarl. Then there were the times he came to Billy's room at night, and did things that he told Billy that if he ever told anyone else about he would kill him.

Things hadn't been like this before his mum had left. She hadn't even said goodbye. One morning she'd been there, sitting on the sofa in that faded pink dressing gown, a mug of tea that she would sip so slowly it must have been cold by the time she'd finished it. Then Billy had come home from school one day to find his dad chucking his mum's things into a huge bonfire, which had continued to burn till late that night. The dressing gown had been the last thing thrown on the fire, and Billy had watched transfixed as the flames slowly engulfed it, surprised at how long it took the cheap fabric to burn.

There were times when Billy really missed her. A great gulf of loss would suddenly hit him in the most mundane of circumstances, during a maths lesson at school, walking down the street, when he closed his eyes at night. Tears would prick his eyes then, though Billy refused to submit to them completely. He had a feeling, strong and overwhelming, that if he started he might never stop, and then his dad would be there, his fist ready.

But tonight he would not be lying on his bed thinking about his mum. He was going out and he couldn't help feeling a quiver of excitement about it.

Simon and his gang were admired and hated in equal measures at school. Everybody, including a couple of the quieter teachers, was afraid of them, and there was a general feeling that the boys were better to have as friends rather than enemies. All three of them lived on that new estate on the edge of town, the posh one, with its long drives and smart perfect gardens. It was a place to aspire to, though Billy dismissed any thoughts of himself ever living there as pointless, an unachievable feat. The trio would often boast about their latest acquisitions, their laptops, their tablets, and they always had the newest mobile phones. Billy would remain at the back of the classroom, watching and listening to it all enviously. There was talk of holidays too, places that Billy had heard of, and were always a plane ride away. Billy didn't know if he'd ever 'been away'. On a couple of occasions, he'd been shipped off to his nan's, who had lived in the next town. But Billy had never classed that as any kind of holiday; in fact, he found it more of an ordeal. She had the same brooding manner as his dad, and a similar relentless smoking habit. She had no desire to talk about his mother either, only once had she been referred to, and then as 'that woman' and she had grimaced.

The boys had always been particular about who they talked to. A number of Billy's class had been the brunt of their name-calling or bullying. Billy couldn't help but secretly admire the way the trio gained a peculiar respect among his fellow classmates, even if it was just out of fear. Billy had until recently been in the 'just don't even bother with him' category. But he had become suddenly determined, especially since his mum left, not to be ignored any longer. He had begun his campaign a few weeks back, and at times it had bought no rewards at all, bar a relentless series of lunchtime detentions. But gradually, it seemed his behaviour began to become noticed by Simon, who had only a week ago nodded and grunted an 'alright' as the pair had passed each other in the corridor. Then came the invitation to a night out trick or treating, and Billy couldn't help hitting the air with an imaginary punch of jubilation when he supposed nobody was looking.

Right now he occasionally glanced at the clock in anticipation whilst studying his dad, who after a few minutes finally lifted himself out of the armchair, stubbing out the butt of his second cigarette in ten minutes. Billy only relaxed when the front door was slapped shut, and his dad's battered Mondeo started up and drove away.

Billy heard them before the doorbell was even rung. It was Simon's voice mainly, the two other boys only occasionally answering with a grunt or a swift 'ok'. He'd been sitting on the stairs, tapping his foot impatiently, feeling peculiarly anxious. Though Billy knew they were there, the high pitched shrill of the bell still made him jump, and he lurched eagerly to the door, opening it just enough so the boys could see his face.

'You ready? Got your mask?' Simon had his balanced on the top of his head, with the two other boys peering behind, scowling like a couple of gargoyles. Billy snatched up the mask that he had put there ready on the side table by the front door. He had bought the mask the other day with money he'd stolen out of his dad's coat pocket, and which he continued to smart with guilt about.

As the four of them walked up the street, it was Simon who did the talking, explaining what they were going to do. The two other boys continued to ignore Billy, but he felt their presence behind.

'We need to get out of this dump,' Simon said. 'I wouldn't eat any of the crap they'd dish out anyway.' Billy hoped that Simon didn't see the awkward look he gave, but he was sure that the other boys did, as he heard one of them snigger. He felt his cheeks burn; Simon was talking about the estate where he lived.

The four boys headed to the better end of town. Billy couldn't help but stare disbelieving at some of the houses. He hadn't been there before. Many of the houses were set far back from the road, their gardens as big as Billy's entire house, and he wondered what sort of people lived in such vast places. They all turned into the small cul-de-sac, where two tall cast iron gates announced the entrance, and the gates suddenly reminded Billy of the ones outside the prison his dad had been sent to a few years ago. All the gardens in the street were well kept, and looked like something from those fancy magazines, and each driveway had a shiny car or two. Billy felt more than a twinge of envy, yet he just couldn't picture himself living in such a place.

They only approached the houses that had pumpkins carved with jeering faces outside or other signs that they were buying in to the spirit of Halloween. Billy was nervous at first, and stood a little further back from the gang of three, wondering if the occupants would turn their noses up at him. But all four of them were greeted with cheers and fake boos, often younger children hiding behind the legs of their parents but staring fascinated all the same. And, the boys had been right in their promise that all four of them would get plenty of treats. They all scooped up handfuls from bowls thrusted eagerly towards them. Billy had never owned so much chocolate, and secretly tucked handfuls into various pockets, promising himself that he could save it for the weeks ahead.

They eventually headed towards another part of town that Billy didn't recognise. He couldn't help but look nervously over his shoulder. The other three suddenly halted outside a house that was set apart from the rest, drenched in darkness, bar a small light that flickered weakly from a room somewhere in the house.

'So Billy Boy ...' Simon now stood menacingly in front of Billy, the two others taking their usual positions at either side of their leader. It was too dark for Billy to make out their expressions, but he guessed they were wearing those peculiar smiles on their faces, as if they knew something but had no intention of sharing it with Billy. 'We've been pretty good to let you join us tonight,' Simon continued and Billy shifted uncomfortably. There was a tone in Simon's voice that he didn't quite trust, and suddenly he wanted to be back in the security of the cul-de-sac, bathed in the comforting light that oozed from the houses there.

'Yeah, we don't let just anybody come, you know.' It was the shorter of the other two boys, Alex. He finished his statement with a snort of derision.

'So, perhaps you'd like to show us how grateful you are?' It was Simon speaking again. It was still a little dark to see Simon's face, but Billy again imagined a smirk slowly growing on his lips.

Billy looked behind him. He wished he had the guts to run home, if he could find his way. But the three of them stood there, a barrier to his freedom and he knew that even if he could get away without them catching him, there would be consequences for him the next day at school if he got away. It would be easier to do what they said.

'See that house,' Simon said, 'that bitch in there shut the door in my face last year. She needs to be taught a lesson in respect.' It seemed Simon had been simmering over this for a whole year. 'And she's weird as well. I've seen her, doesn't even wear shoes. My dad says she's funny in the head.'

Billy realised now why they had let him come tonight. He swore under his breath. How could he have been so stupid? Why on earth would somebody like Simon want to be friends with somebody like him? He blinked away a tear that threatened to escape. Why did nothing good happen in his life? He suddenly heard his dad words, 'You stupid little shit, nobody wants you do they?' That's why Mum had left wasn't it? Because of him; because she'd been disappointed that he wasn't quite the son she had wanted. What kind of kid wanted to sit in his room and read, instead of playing football outside? He hadn't even protected her against Dad. He was pathetic.

Billy turned the stone in his hand. Break a window, that's what Simon had said, that was all he had to do. He had begun to sweat in his coat. The sweets he had eaten now seemed to swirl like a whirlpool in his stomach. He wanted to be sick.

'Get closer.' It was Simon, egging him on, an excitable tone to his voice that made it seem all high pitched and girlish. He heard the snort from one of the other boys. Billy shuffled as slowly as he could forward, hoping it might buy him a little time, but he knew that, deep down, he wouldn't be able to talk himself out of it.

He lifted his arm up and threw the stone as hard as he could.

The sound of glass made him jump, though Billy knew that it was coming. He heard Simon hiss, 'Shit, he's done it.' and then the sound of them running away. For some reason Billy remained with his feet stubbornly fixed to the ground beneath. He looked back for a second, hoping that he would see the other boys, but they had disappeared completely out of view. When he looked back round he was face to face with her, and two hands grabbed him roughly.

Billy was shaking. His eyes stung with discomfort at the bright light that shone from a solitary bulb above his head, but at least he was now able to see the person that had dragged him inside. The woman was no taller than him, but three times as wide. Her hair was short, and it stuck up in odd grey tufts over the head, some bits longer than the others, giving the impression she cut it herself. Her skin was puffy and shallow, the wrinkles etched deep upon it, so that it looked as if her skin hung on the face in folds. The eyes, small and piggy, were bright, excitable, yet her mouth was drawn into a grimace.

'You little bastard.'

Billy was too frightened to move. He had backed himself up against a wall, and it was there he stood nervously, his body pressed up ever harder against it. She paced in front of him in a circle, her hands curled up into fists. Momentarily they would relax, only to tense up in to fists again. It reminded Billy of Dad. He squeezed his eyes shut, anticipating the familiar feeling of physical pain, telling himself he mustn't cry until he was on his own.

But minutes, or what felt like them, passed, and nothing happened, so Billy opened his eyes again.

She was stood in the opposite corner, like a child that had done something naughty. Billy could hear that she was still muttering, but it didn't appear that she was as angry as she had been before.

'I'm sorry. It's a trick. The other boys ... I had to.' She was silent then. He gulped back a sob that had been slowly bubbling up and now threatened to erupt.

'You know nothing about tricks.' Her voice was calm now, but there was some menace behind it. Strangely it made Billy more frightened than if she had yelled out. His dad was the same, sometimes; the placid tone that belied a punch about to be thrown, or sharp painful slap across the ear.

The old woman turned around slowly then, shuffling towards him. She smelt funny. Billy wrinkled up his nose, something earthy which invaded his nostrils, and gradually slid down his throat until he couldn't taste or smell anything but it. He stared into her eyes. They seemed to blacken, and, though he was frightened, he could not draw himself away from these dark glistening pools.

'You like terrorising old women, eh?' Billy shook his head. 'What would your dad say, eh, if I told him?' Billy's bottom lip began to tremble, not just at the thought of what his dad would do to him, but because the old woman seemed to know exactly what lay in store for him in that direction. Why had she not threatened him with the police, or said his parents rather than his dad?

'Please, I'll do anything, just don't.' He mind was running over the beating he would get. It was then the tears began to fall, and he sank down to the floor, a dishevelled heap, gripping his knees, rocking to and fro.

Billy wasn't sure how long he'd been there - eventually though, he couldn't cry anymore and bleary-eyed he looked up at the woman. The eyes, black still, bright and on edge like some kind of trapped animal, remained glaring down at him.

'Come on, get up.' She gestured and Billy a little reluctantly stood to his feet, wiping his face with the back of his sleeve.

She had sat him down in the kitchen and placed a mug in front of him. 'Drink,' she ordered, and Billy, still a little afraid, lifted up the mug obediently and sipped at its contents. It had a peculiar taste, herby, not so dissimilar to what he had smelt from her, but it was not so unpleasant, and after all that crying his throat was sore. 'So what happened to your friends?' The woman stared, and Billy noticed that her lips were now almost curling into a smile.

'There not my friends,' Billy said with a certain determination. He wondered where Simon and the two other boys were now. He imagined them heading back to their estate, laughing, looking forward to hearing about the trouble Billy had got into.

'I guess not.' She unexpectedly winked at him, and Billy wrinkled up his brow.

'Am I going to get into trouble?' He looked up at her then nervously, thinking about his dad, and the thought made him queasy all over again.

'Well, I don't appreciate my window getting smashed, but I didn't get a chance to give you that treat did I?'

Billy gulped down the rest of his tea.

Billy had crashed into several bits of furniture, even with the woman shining the torch in his direction. He had pushed the piece of board awkwardly up against the broken window, and wondered if it would stay there till morning. He had his doubts, but continued with his task anyway.

'I don't use this room much, got all my bit and bobs from the old days here,' she had wistfully sighed. Billy noticed that he could smell the same herb that had been in his tea, it permeated the room, stronger in one corner, remaining in the air like a cowering child. It wasn't unpleasant, and didn't irritate his nose as it had done before.

'I'm sorry about the window.' Billy looked up. He was ashamed about it. She wasn't bad really, an old woman on her own, not much money, unlike Simon with his fancy clothes and latest gadgets.

She shrugged her shoulders. 'Those other boys egged you on I bet. You're not like them, are you though?'

Billy shrugged. She was right, it didn't matter what he did, what lengths he would go to, he and Simon's little gang would never be friends. Billy would always be the butt of their jokes, the weak link, forever trailing behind them.

'Those sort of people always think they can get what they want, little shits,' she cackled. Again she seemed to betray a knowledge of people she didn't know that unsettled Billy.

'Well, he's well off. I suppose you can do what you like when you're rich.'

'Rubbish!' the woman exclaimed and again sniggered

to herself. The forcefulness of her exclamation made Billy jump, and some more of the nervousness with which he had initially greeted her returned.

They returned to the kitchen, and the woman put the kettle on the hob to boil some more water. 'Money might make some people's world go round, but there are higher powers always at work.' she said pouring water into the well-used teapot, as that herby smell filled the kitchen again.

'You mean God?' Billy stared down at the mug she had presented him with, studying the floating leaves.

'Perhaps. There are other spirits though, forces just as strong.' She had placed a mug in front of herself too, and now was looking just as contemplatively into its contents. 'Did those boys tell you what they call me around here?' She looked up then and Billy shook his head vigorously. 'They say I'm a witch.' She remained staring at Billy, watching him keenly, and she was smiling quite broadly now.

'Why aren't you on your broomstick then, it's Halloween?' They both unexpectedly began to laugh then, and Billy took a sip of his tea.

'Getting a bit old to be rushing around in the cold my boy, nicer to conjure up my spells in the comfort of my own home.' Billy smiled wistfully as she spoke. He felt suddenly tired. He balanced his chin on his hands, before he was encouraged to take a few more sips. 'So my boy, what spell would you like if I was a witch, eh? What would you want me to do?' He had shut his eyes now. They had become too heavy to keep open.

'I'd make Simon and his little gang pay, that's for sure.' Behind his closed eyes he suddenly imagined Simon's face disfigured, ugly, the two the other boys screaming and yelping in pain, it made him smile.

'Is that all boy? Come on, you may never meet a real

witch again.' Billy thought about his Dad now. Sitting in his armchair, a cigarette lit, bringing it slowly to his lips and inhaling, a curl of smoke escaping from a nostril, creeping towards him.

Billy thought that he was dreaming. He didn't quite know how he got onto his bed, but there he appeared to be lying until he dawned on him that this wasn't his room at all. That scent, earthy and sweet, was everywhere. It was dark, but there was a slight movement of light above his head; he supposed it might be a candle. It flickered as if there were a breeze disturbing it. He was cold too, his hands painful at the tips, but he just couldn't move. Billy heard the voice too, a chant of words he just couldn't understand, and perhaps they weren't even in English. Like a lullaby, the same phrase over and over again, one voice, then it seemed like lots of voices, back to the single voice again. Billy just couldn't quite decipher if there was one other person in the room, or a crowd. But he found that he was closing his eyes again; he couldn't keep them open, no matter how hard he tried.

When Billy awoke he found himself on a strange bed. He gripped the blankets beneath him; they were too real for it to be a dream. Still a little dazed, he stumbled up the hallway, finding himself at the kitchen, the same kitchen he and the old woman had sat in that night. It was empty now and in the cold light of the day appeared as if nobody had been in it for months.

Billy was late and arrived at the gates of the school out of breath and red faced. Mr. Hargreaves looked disapprovingly over his thin rimmed glasses at Billy.

'William, where is your uniform?'

Billy muttered something about it being in the wash, and ran inside. He paused outside the classroom. The sound of the class, laughing, chattering, suddenly sent a shiver down his spine. He imagined Simon and his little gang at their usual place in the front. They would have walked home last night, laughing to themselves, thinking that they had got him into trouble, knowing that they had one over on him. He took a huge breath; well he'd show them. He looked down at last night's clothes, his knees dirty where he had collapsed, and he tried to brush away the soil, though it now had stained the fabric.

Once in class Billy was surprised to find that Simon and his two friends were not there. Instead, rumours were flying round the school - something serious had happened; there was talk that Simon would never be seen again. By lunchtime, with the head of the school apparently well aware of the rumours that were all anyone was talking about, a special assembly had been called for the whole school to attend. At it, it was announced that there had been an accident the previous night and that Simon Harding had died. His parents, with whom the head had spoken that morning, had agreed that it was best that the whole school should be informed immediately. Bereavement counsellors were to be available for anyone deeply affected by Simon's death. Alexander Ward and Connor Bennett had also been injured in the accident, but their injuries were not expected to be life-threatening.

Billy took little more than this basic information in. The details of the accident drifted over his head as he fought back a wave of nausea. All he could think about was the old woman, and all he could taste in his mouth was the taste of the peculiar tea he had drunk. The taste wouldn't go away. He couldn't get rid of it. Once out from the assembly he didn't want to speak to anyone. He locked himself in one of the toilets, and sat crouched upon the closed seat hugging his legs, for he didn't know how long, before he realised he had to get out of the school. If he was found acting like this, he'd be questioned by a teacher who however well-meaning might force him into talking about the old woman and then they'd think he was mental, or worse they'd start talking about counsellors, or worse yet they'd want to contact his dad and get him taken home. He found the courage to walk himself out of the school and to walk the streets in a daze until it was time that he could go home without it looking like he'd been skipping school. Would his dad have noticed he hadn't come home last night?

The door wasn't locked when he got home, and as Billy let himself in he immediately noticed his dad's trainers laying by the stairs, where he usually threw them most nights, and his worn-out jacket slung carelessly on the stairs. Billy found it almost comforting, but there was a strange smell in the air, like somebody had been roasting meat, and he hadn't smelt that in a long while. He looked intriguingly into the kitchen, the door to which was wide open, but the room had been left pretty as much as it was the other night, and there were certainly no signs that anybody had been preparing dinner in there. Perhaps his dad had come home in a better mood than he had left last night. Sometimes he bought a takeaway and Billy would scavenge what was left. Billy followed the scent to where it was the strongest. It smelt more like burnt meat to him now.

Billy could not scream, though he wanted to. The sound stuck in his throat, as if it were a hard ball that was so constricting he let out his breath in heavy, laborious gasps. He had shut his eyes, but the image remained there, etched like a tattoo on the inside of his eyelids. His dad was in his armchair, perhaps asleep, he would never know as the lump of burnt flesh and fabric that he now was gave no detail away. It seemed that he had made no attempt to move, that when his body had caught fire, his dad had merely sat there and let it happen. A packet of cigarettes lay close by, and what remained of the hand seemed to reach out, much as it did in life, for the next one.

Billy knelt down, his stomach convulsing. He tasted it again then, that herb, stronger than before. Eventually, he forced his fingers down his throat and gagged.

The Dead

Red suits her and she knows it. I could see that as she walked into the bar, the way she carried herself, like a butterfly among the brown, stuttering moths. And the most apt of colours for a woman of her profession, a scarlet woman as my mother would have said. Of course, they dress it up nowadays. Escort. Sounds rather professional, doesn't it? Has a sophisticated ring. She would have recoiled in horror if I had called her a prostitute; she doesn't quite see herself like that does she? She's not a streetwalker, some common little slapper who's giving blow jobs to pay for her next fix. She's a woman who has chosen to do something she knows she is rather good at. She's honest, unlike the hundreds who go out and do just the same for a dinner and a piece of jewellery. A simple transaction, isn't it so? An exchange, a fee for services rendered. You can't get fairer than that, can you? She's looking now, searching around the bar for the client she is booked to see. Ah, there you go, she spots the white rose stick pin in my lapel, my take on the cliché. She begins to smile, trying her best to ignore the admiring glances as she walks steadily to me. Failing dismally.

We kiss, like we know each other. I suppose the shaking of hands would be too formal for this occasion. Lips only lightly touching the skin, nothing more. I can see she is disappointed. Perhaps this happens every time, that she hopes that one day she'll meet the man that will take her away from all this. Somebody rich of course, who will see past what she is. Of course, this is never going to happen. Men who hire her aren't interested in such things. They have their wives; what she offers is something else, temporary, as fleeting as the pleasure one gets from a good cigar or a glass of wine. She is to be enjoyed, but temporarily, and stubbed out like the remnants of that cigar when done. I think she knows this, but still she clings to the fantasy, perhaps it gets her through the darkness that probes the crevices of her mind when she closes her eyes.

But she hides it well, this disappointment. Eyes now to the bar, an indication that perhaps it would be nice if I at least offered to buy her a drink.

Her name is Melissa. Perhaps this is her real name, because she says it with some degree of confidence, but then she is well practised in the art of deceit. She doesn't look like a Melissa. I imagine her with a traditional kind of name, as there is something old- fashioned in her looks. Pre-Raphaelite perhaps might be the word, not quite the beauty that today's society would class as pretty, but, I would say, if you'll forgive my archaic turn of phrase, she is a handsome woman, a refined kind of beauty. She's wearing contact lenses; her eyes are glassy and one a little red just under the rim of the lid. Not that I would have minded glasses; on some women they add an air of intellect that I'm rather fond of, the promise of some decent conversation. I would put her around thirty, though she could, to someone with a less trained eye, pass as being younger. It's the eyes that are ironically the giveaway to her age, well, more the small lines that have begun their journey into her skin, that become a little more defined when she smiles. There are several around the mouth too, an ex-smoker my mind supposes. But she wears her skin well, and she looks like the kind of woman who would retain her looks against the advancing years.

'So Melissa, are you a local girl?' She looks nervously at me at this question. She isn't sure what she should say. She could merely brush it off, but be in danger of being rude or ignorant. On the other hand, if she answers it, she is giving a bit of herself away.

'Yes, I suppose I am.' Good answer. Enough. Again she smiles. I would believe it, if I remained staring at the mouth, red and glistening, but the eyes tell a different story and it's nothing to do with her contact lenses.

I order her a dry white wine as she requests. My empty glass is refilled, but soon emptied again. Vodka, no ice, no mixer, knocked back quickly and without much pleasure. Not a lot gives me that any more. She sips slowly, not enjoying it much either. Perhaps she would have preferred something stronger, but she has this image to portray. The wine, the glass held delicately, is part of that illusion.

We make small talk for a moment while she drinks. Whether it's the wine, I wouldn't like to guess, but she has certainly relaxed since my first question to her.

'And you, you're not local are you?' she says to me at one point. She has noted the accent. I thought I had spent enough time here for the low tones of my French upbringing to have completely disappeared. I have ceased to hear it myself, but other people, strangers, sometimes mention it. There is sometimes a glimmer of excitement, as if they have discovered something unusual, an exotic bird among the pigeons of London. Once upon a time I suppose I would have believed myself to be a Frenchman. But that past is so far away. I have been to so many cities that it seems my childhood years are those of another person's life. As if I had read about them in a book.

'I was born just outside Paris.' This is not a lie. But the

village in which I spent my early years is some considerable distance from the capital, but so obscure that she certainly would not have heard of it. I wonder if it is still there, or has grown into a bustling town. But I have fought the urge to find out. I suppose I like to keep it as it is in my mind; there is comfort sometimes in the memory I have there. If I were to see how it was today, I might not like it.

Melissa is intrigued. I am little surprised by this as London is certainly cosmopolitan, and it is hardly rare for someone living in the capital to have been born abroad. Moreover, she must surely have had clients of many different nationalities. But, her eyes had lit up when I mentioned Paris. Again that fantasy perhaps; she imagines strolling down the more fashionable streets of that romantic city, dining at those restaurants that line the many streets and drinking champagne. She is not quite the hardened tart she likes to portray. And often the mask slips, and she is like a child who still believes in Father Christmas.

'So how long have you been here, David?' I've got her now. She is sipping at her wine, her shoulders have relaxed, in fact her whole posture has, and she leans towards me provocatively.

'For a great many years.' I smile then, leaning towards her, giving the impression that I'm equally as relaxed in her presence. The answer I gave is true; though I still have the deep traces in my voice of my French upbringing, it's a great many years since I have been on French soil. I have been in London for a long time now. Unlike the other cities I have encountered, it is this particular city that has always enthralled me and in which I have felt the most comfortable. I have some English blood in me of course, from my mother. Perhaps that is why I feel at home here, but I feel it's more a question of instinct. I tend to go with my instincts, and so far they have served me well.

'I've never been here before. It's nice.' She laughs, sips at her wine once more. I'm not sure whether this is a lie or not, whether it is just part of the routine that she performs on a regular basis. I wonder, being a curious man, whether perhaps she is ashamed of her past. I wonder what lies beneath the perfectly make-upped face, the heavy kohl eyes.

We talk for a while about nothing in particular. At one point she smiles, coyly turns her head and studies me. Perhaps she is beginning to find me attractive. I know I don't possess Hollywood good-looks, but I have a certain old fashioned charm that has served me well throughout the years.

The conversation eventually turns to business; as it must do. I have paid an hourly outcall rate to the agency, but it is not for the agency to arrange 'extras'. Those arrangements are for me to make directly with Melissa.

'Do you have a room booked?' she says.

'Yes, at the Palace Hotel round the corner. Do you know it?'

She nods, possibly exposing an earlier lie about not having been here before. Perhaps I had been fooled for a moment, taken in by that smile. In my mind I had made up a little story for myself that we had glanced over at each other at our separate tables. Me, as usual on my own, she stood up by some stupid boyfriend and having a commiserative drink before she faced going home alone. Of course, the reality was that I'd searched online for an escort agency that clearly signalled payment for sex was possible. It wasn't a hard thing to find. On the phone to the agency, they all but confirmed in as many words that my escort would be a prostitute. I'd specifically requested a more mature woman than the girls still in or just out their teens whose pictures dominated some of the escort agency websites. Melissa, I was told, would be everything I wanted.

Our business talk concluded, Melissa smiles. Practised, eyes glassy and cold. We leave the bar.

At the hotel she waits patiently behind me as I check in. I am greeted not by the smiling face of a young woman that I might have expected, but a dour man in his forties who barely looks up from the computer screen before handing me the key card and wishing me, in monotone, that I enjoy my stay. We look at each other, just for a moment, but there is something sad about those eyes of his. I wonder if he lives alone, as he has the air of a man missing something. Perhaps it's my age, but I find myself making up stories about the people I encounter. With him, Jim his name badge states, I imagine he is somebody who is disappointed with how life has turned out. Perhaps once upon a time as a young man he had desires, ambitions, but like the flakes of dried skin that have fallen and rest on each of shoulders, those dreams have crumbled and are discarded.

'Thank you, Jim,' I say, for some reason feeling the need to call him by his name.

He smiles a little, then catches sight of Melissa and then stares at me. There is envy in his look; for a moment he wishes he was me with this beautiful woman beside him. But she has come at a price, and so has this life I am living.

The room is clean, but plain. Melissa betrays a look of disappointment at it, I can tell, but she quickly recovers. The smile is there again, then the polite request if she can use the bathroom. She is in there a few minutes, I suppose giving herself a pep talk in the mirror, gritting her teeth, promising herself that it will be over before she knows it.

Placing my shoes by the side of the bed, I slip my jacket off also, hanging it on the back of the chair, where it will patiently wait. I stare up at the ceiling wondering how many eyes had studied its slightly imperfect surface. Melissa has slipped almost silently out of the bathroom. Her presence only announced quite subtly as she unzips her dress and lets it fall to the floor. She stands for a moment, for me to admire I suppose, poised statuesque in the middle of the room. Her underwear is as perfectly applied as her make-up. I have to admit to myself that she is good at this, and I encourage her to come and join me on the bed.

That hand. She is letting it wander, caressing the surface of my skin until I hiss when she lingers longer that she should at the base of my stomach.

'I'm sorry, are you in pain?' She frowns, but quickly recovers when I shake my head and she continues with her exploration. I had freshly packed the wound that morning, like I do every day. It refuses to heal, and festers like a piece of rotting fruit. It no longer bleeds. Instead it oozes yellow, foul smelling pus that stains the wads of cloth I pack it with. Flesh that refuses to heal. The hand travels down, I feel myself stir, but I know I'm incapable, my cock remaining as flaccid and unmoving as my heart.

She asks, 'Is there something that you prefer, something you would like me to do?' There is hesitancy in the voice, and I wonder what answers she has got in the past.

'Do you enjoy this Melissa?' I say. 'I mean really do you want to continue like this?'

She studies me then, her hand poised. 'Of course.' But there is hesitancy in that voice, the mouth trembling and the eyes revealing a truth that only a man like me can read.

'There is no need to lie to me, is there?' I turn and frown at her confusion. 'How long is since you actually felt joy, I mean real joy?'

Melissa turns away, sits up abruptly. 'I've never thought about it, I suppose,' she answers eventually, her back to me and shoulders slumped. She is thinking about it now, trying desperately to grasp some past remembered joy and pull it towards her, like a strand of hair.

I don't remember when I last felt it. I mean the sort of happiness that seeps right down inside and consumes every bit of you. Like the first time you fall in love, or seeing your first born for the first time. I see it in others sometimes, and there is a venomous anger that builds up inside me. Emptiness is more unbearable than pain. Pain is a reminder that you are alive, that you still can feel. Like bleeding.

'Look, I don't mean to be rude,' she says, 'but, well, what do you want, just to talk?'

I smile at this. It's a peculiar concept for her I bet. 'I'm paying you; you asked what I would like, and perhaps, Melissa, I would like to talk.'

She tenses then, hands gripping the edge of the duvet, in anxiety or anger I'm not sure. It is peculiar, but not so unbelievable that she finds this very simple act of holding a conversation more difficult than fucking me. 'Of course, no problem.' That smile, flashed quickly, she's trying desperately to regain her composure.

'So, why don't I find out a little bit more about Melissa, then?'

She turns to me nervously then. The smile remaining, but the eyes give it away. There is a look of fear, a feeling that the pair of us are slipping into uncharted waters. 'There is not much to tell, I'm afraid.' I can see she doesn't want to indulge me. There is a part of her, I guess she wants keep away from all this, which she keeps tucked away in a drawer in her mind that is kept securely locked whilst she is working.

'Really, I would imagine you have a great many stories.'

She purses her lips. 'Maybe, but this time is about you,

about me doing what you like the most, about giving you pleasure.'

She's good, I grant you that. I sit up too quickly, and wince as I feel the wound split a little, that weeping hole widening even more. 'Perhaps we should have a little drink.' I inspect the contents of the room's minibar. It has vodka and scotch miniatures, mixers and a bottle of white wine, along with beer and soft drinks. I select the bottle of wine and unscrew its cap. She is hesitant, I guess she doesn't allow herself to get too drunk on the job; she is not in control then. But she relents, pours me a glass. I have to admit I just don't enjoy drink anymore. It had ceased to give me the buzz that it had done years ago. Like most things now, I do them out of necessity.

I swiftly empty my glass, letting the wine slide through my rotting body, knowing it will remain swirling around my stomach for hours, like I'm an empty vessel.

'You're not like the other men.' She is sipping at her wine slowly, but I can see the alcohol is having some effect.

'Oh Melissa, I'm not I assure you.' We both smile then.

'I never intended to do this for long, you know, it was a stop gap, after university. But ... I don't know it just seemed harder to stop.'

And now she can't. Like something caged, a rodent on one of those maddening wheels, she has to keep on going.

'It's not all that bad though, I suppose,' she says, before she lunges towards me, the wine she has had unexpectedly taking hold. My wrist is the first bit of me that she reaches and this she grips as if her very life depended on it. She sees it then. Another wound, self-inflicted a life time ago by a younger self and when my body still had the capacity to repair itself. A thin slit, done with a scalpel, so deep it almost went to the bone. There is a matching one, done the same night, as deep and precise as this one. She pauses, caught off guard.

I have imagined the moment that I die so many times, replayed it again and again, as if I am an actor in somebody else's play. I have plunged myself into the river, the Thames itself, and felt its murky, dark contents fill my lungs and seemingly appear to swallow me whole. But I am still here. That wound, the one that refuses to heal I inflicted on myself several months ago with a blunt kitchen knife, feeling with a perverted pleasure the peculiar flatness of the metal against my spongy organs. But though it weeps continuously I remain alive.

Melissa suddenly pulls back, retreating to the chair where she had thrown off her dress. I can see it in her eyes then, and I can't deny that I am disappointed. I will not enjoy this. She was not quite as she seemed.

She fights, desperately, in some vain hope that her desperate clawing at my arms and occasionally my face will stop me, that suddenly I will come to my senses, let her put her clothes on and she can walk out of here. I thought I had chosen well, that I sensed a kindred spirit, but this time the mask that she has worn has worked a little too well.

Most of them welcome my hands around their throat. Some even suggest the way they choose to end their last moments on this earth. Perhaps they believe that this way all will be forgiven and that the pearly gates of their imagined Heaven will open up, accept them in.

I am forced to wrestle her with all the strength I have and to straddle her with my thighs. I am stronger than I look and no amount of struggling will release her. I wonder if her desperate, sudden scream has alerted any of the other guests outside, and I think suddenly of poor sad Jim on the reception desk. And there is a moment, me half listening that she hisses, 'Please ... don't hurt me.'

And I don't, any more than is necessary.

I stare at her for a while. Still beautiful, though the emerging welts of red around her neck spoil the illusion that she is merely sleeping. She fought disappointingly hard and I am left unsatisfied. There is no joy is taking the life of somebody who clearly wants to carry on living, and I am almost feeling a little sorry about it.

I walk among you all, seeking the dead masquerading as the living. I have taken it upon myself to help these poor lost souls on their way, to give them the gift that I have been denied.

Made in the USA
Charleston, SC
06 September 2016